# THE MARRIAGE DARE

PENNY WYLDER

Thanks for Reading!

Sign up for my newsletter and leave
your panties at the door!

**Sign up HERE!**

1
________

## DANIEL

The woman in front of me laughs. Loud and brassy and totally over the top. "And that's why I say never spend too long in a tanning bed, you know? Too many risks." She laughs again, this time placing her hand on my arm.

I laugh along with her, though I don't find her funny. They rarely are. She's only speaking to me because she knows that I'm the owner of this casino and she's hoping that I'm going to fuck her. Take her upstairs and show her a good time so she can get showered in fancy room service and the bragging rights that she fucked the owner of Brazen Casinos. Sometimes I take them up on their offers and show them a good time. But usually those are the ones that have a spark. Something unique about them that makes me want them, at least for the night. Other than truly magnificent size of her implants, this one has nothing. And that's saying a lot, considering how badly I need a good fuck right now.

Most of the women who try to throw themselves at me have done their research. And they know that I don't enjoy speaking with sloppy drunks, and that I never have more than two drinks in an entire evening. She—I can't remember her name—has had two drinks in the course of our thirty-minute conversation. Probably to convince me that she's drunk enough to hit on. But I don't take advantage of people. If there was ever a way to turn me off, that's one of the fastest ways. If she wants to spend her money in my establishment, I'm not going to argue with her. But nothing else is going to happen. Even though she's bragging now about her extensive exercise routine and how *flexible* she is. I struggle not to roll my eyes.

Not that she has any idea that I'm not paying attention in the slightest. She's self-absorbed enough not to notice, and you don't get to where I am without having some charm and the stamina to speak to people that you don't enjoy. Brazen Casinos is the most successful chain in the western United States, and everybody wants a piece of that. Especially here at our flagship in Las Vegas. So I plaster a smile on my face and make wannabe groupies and VIPs feel good about spending their money before they get so drunk that I have my staff take them back to their rooms.

Rinse, repeat.

She'll wake up with a hangover tomorrow, remember this as the best conversation of her life, and wonder what on earth she did to wake up in her own bed before she has to leave for the airport. Oh, and she'll spend another five figures in the casino before she leaves. No skin off my back. I've seen people like her a hundred times, and it's worth it to spend a few minutes listening to vapid conversation for that much profit. Hell, maybe I'll even tell the concierge to give her a ten percent discount on everything. Especially the drinks. In my experience, nothing makes rich women spend money faster than the thought that they're actually saving money.

But fuck, I'm tired. I'm trying to focus on what's in front

of me but my attention keeps drifting to literally everything else. I make a note of a lightbulb over one of the poker tables that's flickering. I'll have to have that changed by maintenance.

I need a vacation. A long one. Which is laughable, given the amount of money I have and the fact that I run a business fueled by vacations. But as many wealthy men know, it's hard to keep your wealth if you don't work. So a vacation isn't in the cards for me right now. I'm poised to open another two locations and I'm not going to risk anything going wrong during the launch of those properties because I couldn't power through. I just need a good night's sleep, and maybe a good fuck—though not with her—and I'll be good as new.

The woman whose name I've forgotten raises her hand to the waitress for another drink, and I pull out my phone. No urgent messages, unfortunately. Nothing to get me out of this. Usually I just let my mind fade into a smooth fog and wait, but this conversation is grating on me. I could flip through my phone and see if there's anyone I feel like calling for that late night booty-call, but after this conversation, even the idea of that isn't appealing.

I take a sip of the whiskey in my glass and savor it, focus on the rich taste. The smokiness. It's the best that money can buy, and not the whiskey that the bar here serves to anyone. It's reserved only for me. But tonight, it's not enough.

But that might be about to change.

Across the room, I see a woman in a blue dress. She's facing away from me, but that doesn't matter—the back of her dress plunges to her waist, giving me one hell of a view. It's a pity that the dress doesn't fall any lower, because even from here, I can see that she's got a fantastic ass. One that I can imagine gripping firmly, and is completely distracting me from the movie in front of me. Dark hair falls in waves over her shoulders of the woman in blue, and she gracefully sits at one of the poker tables.

That's when I notice something else. That dress, gorgeous as it may be, isn't new. A dress like that—and I see many gorgeous dresses walking around my casino—is made for the wearer, and this is not. It's too long. I see her try to sweep it around her chair so that it doesn't get tangled. And the dress gapes a little, giving me a glimpse of the side of her breast.

So she bought it from someone. Not a crime of course, just intriguing. It's not something that a lot of people would notice, because they'd be blinded by her beauty. And it almost worked with me. But I like a little bit of mystery. Most people who come into a Brazen Casino wouldn't be caught dead in second hand clothes. Hell, she's got a body good enough that I know plenty of designers would offer her clothes for free simply to see her wear them.

She's a ways away, so it's difficult to tell, but I think I spy a frayed edge at the hem of the gown. Definitely interesting.

I'm no stranger to hand-me-down clothes. I didn't own a new article of clothing until well into my twenties. But this image doesn't make sense, and figuring out the puzzle of the mysterious brunette is far more interesting than listening to a busty blonde blather about her overseas yoga retreats.

Pulling out my phone again, I activate the security system. We have cameras covering every table, as cheating is one of the worst offenses in my—or any other—casino. But in this instance I'm not looking for cheating. I'm looking for her face.

I flip through the cameras until I find the right table, waiting until she turns. And when she does, my entire body goes cold with shock. I know her. She has a face I'll never forget and crimes against me that I'll never forgive.

Monica Blast. The rich girl from next door who tormented me for years without reason or excuse. I'll never forget her face. Or lose the desire to take revenge. And here she is, not fifty feet away. Only a fool wouldn't see this as an opportunity.

She's on my turf, and wearing clothes that don't suit her. Monica was never a person that had problems with money —she could afford whatever she damn well pleased. So why is she wearing a dress like that? Not that I mind watching the curves of her back. She's been sexy since high school, and she knew it too. I can't imagine that things have changed so much for her that she'd need to rely on hand-me-downs, but I suppose that anything can happen. But there's a small alarm bell ringing in my head.

Another thing that I've learned about rich people: If they lose their money, they'll fight like hell to get it back. Even if that means cheating or stealing. Poor little rich girl in my casino in a dress that screams of lost wealth isn't something that I can just ignore.

It doesn't matter that she's sexy as hell in her second-hand dress. It doesn't even matter why she's here in the first place. What matters is that she took everything from me. I never thought that I would have a chance to pay her back for all the *kindnesses* that she paid me when we were younger. Because of course, attention at all from someone of her 'status' was always a kindness, wasn't it?

I have to hold myself back from laughing, the dark thoughts blooming in my mind. Monica is the woman who made me who I am today. I never stopped fighting to take back what she stole, and now I have everything I could want and more. Except one thing. Revenge.

My mind is fully awake now, revving up and formulating a plan. She deserves everything that's coming to her. Perfect humiliation, and greater pleasure—but only if she begs me for it. I'll fuck her mind before I fuck her body. But I can be sure that I'm going to do both.

The now-drunk blonde is still talking, this time about the absolutely extravagant trip that she took to the Maldives with her girlfriends—and a few of the boy toys they use when their husbands aren't around. Fucking rich people. Seeing Monica reminds me how much I hate people like them, and how even though I'm approaching the stage of near limitless wealth, I'll never, ever, be like them. I stand quickly, knocking back what's left of my whiskey. "Excuse me."

I walk away from her without another thought, leaving her gaping and sputtering because I now have far better things to do.

As I watch Monica flip her hair over her shoulder, a memory comes to me. It's so vivid that I have to stop walking and let it replay. A defining moment between us.

The sun was bright that day. I remember because it shone off her hair. So many details pop out at me from those moments—the smell of the dirt under me after she pushed me down, the sound of her friends laughing, and my panic.

It had been summer, and I worked as a dishwasher at a little diner in our town for almost nothing because I was fifteen and they just needed another body. I had saved every penny from that job, and finally bought myself something. A Game Boy. Rage flies through my chest even now over the stupid, simple object. But it was the most expensive thing that I had ever owned, despite the fact that it was used and more than a little beat up when I got it.

I loved that Game Boy more than anything. Those first

few weeks I had it were the best, the rest of my measly salary going to buy old games to play on it. *Finally*, I had thought *finally, I know what it feels like to be like them*. People with money. People who didn't struggle every day for simple things like Mom and Dad. I had even tried to give them the money I used to buy the toy, but they wouldn't hear of it. They insisted that I use the money to buy something for myself.

My guilt was strong, but I bought the Game Boy, and it was the most fun I'd ever had. Until that day. I'd returned from my shift at the diner and was playing a game on the porch when Monica and a few of her friends came down the street. My parents were still at work—they were almost always at work. She had been mean to me for a long time, but lately she had been nicer. I smiled and waved as they passed.

"Hi, Daniel," Monica said. "What are you doing?"

I shook my head. "Nothing much, just playing a game."

"Can I see?" She had sounded so genuinely curious, and she had been so beautiful. Perfect pink sundress waving in the breeze. Of course I said yes, and sprinted down off the porch to show her. I showed her the game. It was something simple, I barely remember now. It's not one of the details that's preserved.

Her friends laughed when I showed them, and then, she did too. "What a nerd," one of them whispered.

Monica was still laughing. "I've never seen you with a Game Boy before."

"I just got it," I told her, still oblivious. "I've got a job washing dishes at Joe's."

One of the friends rolled their eyes. "No you don't. I go to Joe's every week and I never see you there. He probably stole it."

"I do work there," I protested. "Customers can't see into the back where I'm working."

"He definitely stole it," the other friend said, stepping in front of Monica. "Why are poor people always such filthy liars? Aren't they, Monica? Filthy liars."

"Yeah," Monica said quietly, appraising me. She isn't looking at me with the same hatred as the other two, but neither is it kind.

"I—" I didn't even get the chance as I was shoved to the ground. The dirt was hot under me, and I could smell it.

"Don't even bother," the first girl said, yanking the Game Boy out of my hands. "People like you don't deserve stuff like this." She handed the toy to Monica. "You should break it to teach him a lesson."

Monica took it, and she was still staring at me. Her eyes were cold and completely devoid of emotion. There was silence for a moment, like she was waiting for something, though I didn't know what. Why was she doing this? Why were any of them? I thought things were getting better.

And even though I hated this, I couldn't help but notice how gorgeous Monica was. She had grown up, and I was starting to notice curves that hadn't been there before. Curves that I craved to touch.

I was disgusted with myself for wanting her, but that didn't change the pull of desire in my gut or the way I was chanting in my head to try not to get hard. They were already mocking me, I didn't need them to make fun of me for being a pervert too.

"Smash it." One of the girls said.

"Yeah, smash it."

The words went up in a chorus, begging Monica to break the Game Boy, and my heart started to pound. She wouldn't. Not really. Right? I had worked so hard. I hadn't stolen it. There was no reason to break it. I pushed my hands under me and started to sit up, distracted by a shift in her movement.

It was Monica's legs that caught my eye, the way they peeked out from underneath her dress. At the angle I was, I could almost see up it, and I was caught in a moment of indecision about whether to stand because suddenly all I wanted was to see just a little bit further. To see if she was as pink and sexy as I had imagined at night when she plagued my thoughts.

She saw. Monica's eyes narrowed as she looked at me, figuring out exactly where I had been looking, and anger flared on her face. It was the first emotion that she had shown—pure and utter fury. Her friends were still egging her on, begging her to smash my most precious possession, and as I watched, her face turned into a cruel smile.

"Monica," I begged. "Please. Don't."

She did it anyway. I was on my feet in a second but I wasn't fast enough. She threw it with horrifying force into the street, and I watched as it splintered apart into pieces. Her friends cheered and then laughed, and I felt cold steel and anger grow in my chest.

For the briefest of seconds, I thought I saw regret on her face. But it was only for a second as her friends pulled her away, and in the next moment one of them said something that had them all laughing.

It served me right, I remember thinking. I should never have been fooled by her beauty. Monica Blast was my nemesis. It was pure and simple. She was a bully in beautiful packaging and I needed to always remember that. Stuck-up rich princess, and the biggest bitch I had ever known. My enemy. My bully. And in my limited experience, I had found that bullies didn't change.

**2**

---

## MONICA

Don't panic. Do. Not. Panic.

I take a deep breath, in and out to calm my beating heart. I just lost that hand, but I have enough money for a couple more if I play my cards right. Literally. And then I've got nothing. My whole life I've been told about beginner's luck, and I can't think of a time that I needed it more. Turns out, beginner's luck is absolute horseshit.

But never let them see you sweat, right? Pretend you're at a pageant. When I used to walk the stage in beauty pageants, poise was everything. It didn't matter if you tripped or weren't perfect, as long as you were poised. I can do that now. I flash a brilliant smile at the dealer as he deals the cards. The dress I'm wearing is one of my pageant gowns from years past. I found it in one of the boxes and decided to take it for one last spin before I try to sell it. It doesn't fit anymore since I'm thinner from skipping meals and I no longer wear the ankle-breaking heels that are meant to be worn with it.

Sitting in a box hasn't exactly done the dress any favors either, but it's good enough to get by, and that's all I need right now. "How are you tonight?" I ask the dealer. Not to distract him or anything, but because it's easier for me to conceal my nerves if I'm talking.

"I'm doing well," he says quietly. Hands move deftly over the cards as he deals. I peek at my hand, and my heart sinks. It's a two and a three. Not exactly what you want when you're trying to win big.

But maybe not everything is lost, because the card that lands face up on the table is a six. Okay. Okay. Possible straight. I just smile like I've got everything I want in the world, even though I have absolutely nothing. Nothing.

The next card on the table is a four. Holy shit. I mean...it could be. Someone folds, but I don't. It could be that famous beginner's luck kicking in. The universe knows how much I need it. The money I have sitting in front of me is all that I have left, and it's not enough to pay any of the bills that are hanging over my head. But if I won this. That at least would be a start.

Across the table, a man stops to observe the game. He's standing in the shadows, but even from here, I feel a hitch in my chest. He's gorgeous. Dark suit that clings to him like it was tailored within an inch of its life—and in a place like this, it probably was. Broad shoulders and trim waist and enough stubble on his jaw to give an air of insolence even if he's put together like a perfectly designed package.

He's watching our table. Actually, he's watching me. I pretend not to notice and turn on my most brilliant smile. I've got this. This is my hand. I'm going to win it. The universe owes me that much. When the bet comes to me, I push my chips forward. "All in."

The dealer looks at me, and then at cards on the table. "You sure?"

"I am."

He simply shrugs. Only one other person at the table has the guts to go all in with me, but that's too bad, because he's about to lose a lot of money. Across the table I see the handsome man in the shadows smile. God, that smile gives me goosebumps. It's a smile that's meant for darkness and pleasure and whispered words.

I smile back. Maybe this win will make him come talk to me. I think I'd like that. Money and a handsome man to talk to would be a start toward making this day better. Hell, toward making this *year* better.

The dealer burns a card and flips the last one.

It's a seven.

Oh my God.

No.

No, that's not what was supposed to happen! I'm dumbstruck by it, especially when the other man who went all in flips his cards and reveals that he had two spades matching the three on the table. I hadn't even noticed that they were all spades. Shit.

The dread swirling in my stomach is overwhelming, and I watch the dealer reign in all of my chips—the only money I have left, and give it to the man on the other side of the table. But never let them see you sweat. Never.

I flash a smile at the dealer and the rest of the table. "You win some, you lose some. Thank you for the games." And then I step off the chair, careful to gather up the too-long train of my dress so I don't trip, and flee as quickly as possible. I need somewhere to think and breathe. I knew that this was a stupid idea. I *knew* it, and I did it anyway. Because I just needed some kind of hope. I needed to believe that some kind of miracle could happen to get me out of this place I'm in. But miracles aren't real. I might as well have spent that money on lottery tickets for all the good those games did me.

I've known that for a long time now.

Across the casino floor is a bar that's relatively quiet. Dimmer lights and calmer music, generally less frantic than the neon lights and high energy of the rest of the casino. Perfect. I tuck myself onto a stool in the corner where I hope no one will notice me, and I try to take a deep breath.

I don't get very far. It feels like my lungs won't take in air, and tears are threatening to rise up and overwhelm me. What do I do now? I have nowhere to go. Absolutely nothing to my name. The shelters around here are decent, though I never thought that when I did research into them that I'd actually have to take advantage of them. Never.

There's a clink of glass as one of the women behind the bar sets down a glass at my elbow, and I look up, startled. It looks like whiskey. "I didn't order this," I say. Not only did I not order it, there's no way that I can afford it and I don't want to fight with anyone over a bill that I don't owe.

"I know," she says, smiling. "He did." She points to a man standing a few feet away, and I startle. I hadn't even noticed him get that close. But I immediately recognize that he's the handsome man who was watching the poker match that just spectacularly blew up in my face.

He approaches, and I get to see him more closely. What I had thought was handsome turns out to be devastatingly gorgeous. Chiseled jaw with the right kind of stubble—the kind that you want to feel on your thighs. He looks vaguely familiar, but I must be crazy because I'm pretty sure that I would remember someone like him. Any woman with eyes and an imagination would remember that face and put it to good use with her hand between her legs.

There's a little smile on his lips, and he lifts his own

drink in salute. I put on my best beauty queen smile. "Thank you for the drink."

He laughs softly, and it's almost like a purr. I swear that I can feel that sound in my gut, making me long to lean forward to get closer. "You looked like you might need it, after that last hand."

I toss my hair over my shoulder, taking a sip of the whiskey. God, that's good. Definitely top shelf. And goddamn right I need a drink. "I was tired of playing," I say. "I figured I should go out big."

"You were tired of playing after only three hands?" he asks. "I don't think that's true, but you're as cocky as you ever were."

"What?" I'm confused. He's talking to me like he knows me, but I've never been in this casino before. And I'm pretty sure I've never met him before.

He takes another step forward and extends his hand. "I'm Daniel. It's a long time, no see, Monica."

A bunch of things click together in my head, and my mouth literally drops open. Okay. I have seen him before. Have met him. But I haven't seen him in *years*. Not since we were both teenagers. Daniel Argent. The skinny boy who lived next door. I can't say that I was exactly kind to him, even if I wanted to be. But that was a long time ago and things were very, very different then. "Daniel," I say, as I take his hand. "Wow. I...did not expect that."

"No," he says, "I wouldn't think so. Why would you remember somebody like me?"

I flush, embarrassed at his assessment, but I can't exactly disagree with it. I was merciless when I was younger. I thought that the world belonged to me, and I never knew anything about true hardship. That, I've been learning about recently, and the crash course hasn't been fun, though it may have been necessary.

I take another sip of the drink to steady myself. "How have you been?"

"I'm doing all right," he says with a simple shrug of his shoulders. "Brazen is doing very well. I'm very pleased with expansion."

I can't stop the gasp that escapes me. "Brazen? As in *Brazen Casinos*? You own them?"

He nods. "Every last one."

Wow. Okay. "That's amazing. Really. I'm happy you've done so well for yourself."

"Are you?" he asks, tilting his head. "The Monica I knew wouldn't be pleased about that. Though from the state of that dress, you're not exactly the Monica I used to know."

The blush is in full force on my face and I have to look away from him. "What's wrong with my dress?" The words come out softly, and I'm not sure I *want* to know what he has to say about my appearance, but I suddenly can't stop myself. I *need* to know.

"I grew up poor. I can see a dress that doesn't belong to you. It doesn't fit. It's too long, and the hem is in disrepair. Most women who come into my casino take pride in their appearance."

The words cut deep, and my anger overcomes my embarrassment. "This dress *is* mine. Just from a long time ago. The Daniel I knew wouldn't judge someone because they were wearing older clothes."

He leans closer, eyes burning. "The Daniel you knew took a lot more shit than I do, Princess."

Oh my God. The word princess hits me right in the gut, and even though he's looking at me like I'm the last person in the world he wants to be sitting with, I want him to close the distance. I want him to kiss me. I want to feel his anger transmuted into something deeper, and hotter. He sees it in my eyes, and smiles. When he leans back into his chair, I'm left practically panting with the need for him to come closer again.

"So you need money," he says. "How the mighty have fallen? Never thought I'd see the day when the Blast Dynasty wanted for anything."

I freeze. "So you don't know what happened?"

"No. Tell me."

"I'll save my breath. One google search will tell you what you need to know."

He raises an eyebrow, but pulls out his phone and reads. I know exactly what he'll find. That my father, Andrew Blast, the famous real estate mogul and hedge fund genius, was pulling shady shit. Cutting corners and endangering people's lives with the construction he built, and all in order to save money. As far his investments, they were all a sham, most of the money going into his pocket. He did it for years. The construction business caused millions of dollars in damage, maybe more. Thousands of people lost their retirements and livelihood because they invested with him.

My father is in jail now, but in a prison that might as well be a country club. He turned over the names of a lot of people to make a deal with the federal agents investigating him, and in return he gets to live out his sentence in a place that's a glorified hotel. My family's entire fortune is gone, covering the thousands of lawsuits and settlements. Fixing the safety issues he created in his buildings and rebuilding the life savings of people far worse off than we ever were. His decisions have led to the death of over 100 people, and even though I had nothing to do with any of it, it destroyed my life.

My law degree is utterly worthless because no one will hire me. No one wants a Blast working for them, and it's too late to change my name and start over. The damage has been done. I don't even blame them. I have a recognizable face due to my stint on the pageant circuit and the fact that my father was known across the country. Unless I undergo massive plastic surgery, I'm left with the reputation that he left me.

My mother basically went into hiding. I have no idea where she is, and haven't heard from her in years. I miss her, even though she wasn't the best mom. I don't blame her for any of this. She was a victim too. I truly believe that.

So now I'm jobless, about to be homeless, broke and sitting in a casino with a man who I tortured when we were kids. And he's now rich and sexy as fuck. As an objective observer, I don't see how this situation could get any worse.

Daniel's eyes flick back up to mine, appraising me in the light of the new information that he now has. "I'm surprised that I didn't hear about this."

"So am I," I say. "I feel like everyone has at this point. More people than you can count feel the way that you do—they're thanking God that the Blast Dynasty has crumbled. I'm untouchable now. Everyone hates the Blasts, and I can't find a job anywhere because of what he did."

"What do you do now?"

I sigh, because I've heard the question before from people who knew me when I was young. They expect me to say something vapid and frivolous. But I left that behind a while ago. "I'm a lawyer. Or at least I was attempting to be. I can't even fault people for not wanting me on their payroll. But the result of that is what you see: Monica Blast in an old dress using the last of her money on beginner's luck."

Daniel tilts his head to the side just a fraction, studying me. "I'll make you an offer, if you'll let me."

"An offer?"

"More of a wager," he says, taking a sip of his own drink. I watch the way he swallows, and I never thought that watching that motion could be sexy. But his throat moves, and I want to see what's connected to the rest of him beneath that suit. Daniel is a perfect example why you should never judge someone. If I had had to take bets on who Daniel Argent would turn out to be as an adult, this would not have been it.

In fact, if someone had asked me to describe what I thought he looked like now, I would have thought maybe someone skinnier, with a job in IT. Not a powerful man in a suit who runs—owns—the country's biggest chain of luxury casinos. I have no idea what he's going to offer me, but it's too intriguing of a statement for me not to find out. "What is it?"

He places his glass on the bar slowly. Deliberately. "I'll give you two million dollars if you play a hand of poker with me."

The words startle my spine straight. Two million dollars? That's an absurd amount of money for one game of poker. But it's also exactly what I need. Two million would solve all of my debt, and if I managed it well, allow me to live for years while I figure out how to get rid of the stain attached to my name. "Do I have to win?"

Daniel nods once. "Yes."

"I don't have anything to play with," I say. "As I previously stated, I'm broke. I have nothing. Your dealer over there took the last of my money in that unfortunate hand. I have nothing to offer."

He raises his hand, and the bartender appears again

with a drink identical to the one that I hold in my hand, even though I haven't finished the first one. "Drink that," he nods to the glass in my hand. "You're going to need it when you hear the rest of my proposal, I think."

That doesn't exactly bode well, but I can't say that I actually have a choice right now. I knock back what's left of the whiskey and hand the empty glass to the bartender. The new glass is there waiting for me, but I don't pick it up yet, savoring the burn of the alcohol in my throat. I can feel it settle over me like a blanket. "Okay."

"When you say that you have nothing to offer," Daniel says, "that's not exactly true."

"What do you want?" Nerves sizzle in my gut, because I'm desperate, and he knows that. I'm in the weakest position to strike a bargain.

He smiles, and I try not to get distracted by how fucking sexy he's become. "If you win, you get two million dollars. If I win, you marry me."

A laugh escapes me, and I pull it back. That has to be a joke, right? No one bets marriage on poker. Especially not men as rich as Daniel. Besides, he doesn't even like me. "You're joking?" I notice that he's not laughing with me. His eyes are deadly serious, and he hasn't moved an inch. "Oh God, you're serious," I say. He nods once.

He was right, I do need the drink. I grab the glass and drink it down in one long go, practically begging it to overtake me and make me forget that this is happening and where I am. Daniel chuckles now, because he was absolutely right about me, and we both know that.

A third drink appears at my elbow, and I pick it up, taking a sip but not downing it. I can't go too fast or I'm going to agree to something that I regret entirely. "You want me to marry you?"

"Yes." The answer is simple and direct. No evasion.

"Why?" I can't wrap my head around it. It doesn't make a whole lot of sense to me.

Daniel sighs. "Because I've never stopped thinking about you. You're present in everything I do, and every decision I make. The way you treated me—bullied me—it changed me as a person. It taught me how to survive, and how to be ruthless. And even though you were a horrifying bitch to me, I wanted you. I worshipped the ground that you walked on. I hated myself for wanting you, and I hated you for being so damn appealing.

"And then your father happened. He bought every piece of property in the neighborhood out from underneath people. You had already moved away by then. He had a big corporation on his side, wanted to turn the place into condos. My family didn't have the money to fight it, and the money he offered wasn't nearly enough. We didn't have anywhere to go. We scraped by. I had to drop out of school to help make ends meet. My mother was already in poor health, and the stress of everything, along with moving from place to place so often, ruined her health. He ruined everything."

Guilt clenches in my gut. I know a lot of these stories. I've heard so many from people who want to tell me all the horrible things that my father did. I know the statistics. And I know that there are a thousand other stories like Daniel's. But still, it's different hearing it from someone you grew up with. Who you *knew*.

"But I didn't know your father," Daniel continues. "I just knew you. Perfect Monica Blast who got everything that she wanted while the people around her suffered. And I didn't hate your father—I hated you."

"I'm sorry," I whisper. There's nothing that I'll ever be

able to do to change the past or help the people that my family stepped on. And there's no way I'll ever be able to relieve myself of the guilt, even if I didn't do any of it. "But I still don't understand. If you hate me that much then why do you want me to marry you?"

The way Daniel smiles now is feral. Predatory. I see the ruthless businessman he's become to create a place like Brazen, and it makes me shiver with fear and desire equally. "Like I said. Even though you had a part in ruining my life, it made me stronger. It made me who I am today. My family is well cared for now, and healthy because I've made my fortune. Though I'll admit, I'm still warring myself and my emotions when it comes to you."

Curiosity strikes me. "Oh?"

"I want to thank you, for helping me to forge all this. But I also want to destroy you. I want to take my revenge and show you exactly what you did. I want to fuck you and make you mine and then expose you for the spoiled princess that you are. But no matter what I want, I can't do any of it if you're not with me. By my side. So if you lose, marry me."

My gut has plummeted through the floor. I shouldn't be so fucking attracted to a man who has just said that he wants to own me solely so that he can destroy me and pick me apart piece by piece. But my mind catches on the words that he wants to fuck me and *make me his*. My body reacts to that like I'm being lit on fire, desire dampening between my legs. "Just like that?"

"Just like that," he says. "Become a part of my life."

The way he says it, it's like it's a done deal. But it's not. The other part of it is that it's left up to chance. If I win, I get my freedom. Two million dollars is a lot of money, and even though I just lost that hand, I'm not a complete idiot when it comes to poker.

If I lose...

I have no doubt that Daniel will destroy me. But what choice do I have? Even if he plans to destroy my reputation further, I won't be in a worse position than I am now. And if I'm married to him, at least I'll have a place to sleep.

But first he has to win, and I'm not convinced that he will. Maybe my beginner's luck was being saved for this, because it somehow knew that this was coming and I'd need it more than those other hands. I don't have a choice. It's either this, or I'm sleeping in a shelter by the end of the week.

I take a sip of the whiskey. "Okay," I say. "I'll do it. But only because you're going to lose and your bank account will be two million lighter tonight."

He smirks. "I'll barely notice that it's gone. *If* you win."

"Oh, I will." I say it with a confidence that I don't entirely feel. But I have to stay focused. I can do this, even if I'm feeling those two glasses of whiskey. The universe has dropped a chance in my lap and I'm going to take it.

"We'll see," Daniel says, standing and reaching out his hand for mine. "Let's go."

## 3

# DANIEL

There's more of a buzz running through my veins from Monica's proximity than any of the whiskey that I've had tonight. Now that I made my offer—or set my trap, depending how you think of it—I can't wait to spring it.

I wasn't exactly truthful with Monica. Or rather, I didn't tell her everything. She did contribute to ruining my life, and I do want revenge. But this is more than just a simple hand of poker. Because my family had no money, and we barely had a home, playing cards was one of the only sources of entertainment that I had. Especially after she smashed that Game Boy. To say that I learned poker would be the understatement of a lifetime.

I *breathed* poker. I learned the rules and the statistics of the game. And more than that, I learned how to play the people sitting across from me. Poker is a game of chance, but it's also a game of manipulation. I saw the way she convinced herself that she had just as good chance of winning as losing. But I know better. She doesn't know what she's doing, and she's not walking out of here with two million dollars. If everything goes my way, she won't be walking out of the casino at all.

Poker was the way I made a name for myself. Tournaments between shifts at the auto shop, and eventually enough money to take a chance at the big leagues. I never looked back. I could have retired off of my winnings from poker and taken care of my family for the rest of their lives. But after everything that we went through, "good enough" isn't my style. So I took those winnings and gathered investors and opened the first Brazen Casino. The right idea at the right time.

I lead Monica through the casino toward my private poker suite. I hold high stakes games here for VIPs and friends if they're ever in town. Tonight it will just be Monica and me, and I can't wait. She's even more beautiful up close, and more beautiful than I remember. I did tell her the truth when I told her that I'm at war with myself. Everything in me wants to skip the poker game and take her upstairs and fuck her until she's screaming my name. But I also want to see her brought low. I want Monica Blast to know humiliation and more. I want her on her knees before me—figuratively and literally.

She'll beg me. For every single thing that I can give, she'll beg. I'll treat her like a queen. Shower her with luxury and then take it away. Give her pleasure that's never enough. Until she's crawling after me. Then maybe, once I've decided she's had enough, I'll relent. Maybe.

The vision of her kneeling before me fills my head and I'm glad that I'm walking in front of her because I'm instantly hard. Monica has a gorgeous body and even more beautiful face. Perfect lips that I'm dying to see wrapped around my shaft. I want to see her swallow my cum. I want to look into her eyes and see her powerless in front of me. The boy she used to mock and bully. I want her to *feel* how the tables have turned.

But that will have to wait. I need to focus now, because I have no intention of losing. There's a guard—Devon—at the door to my suite, and he nods to me as I approach. Taking a step back, I place my hand on Monica's bare back—thank God for the way this dress is built—and usher her inside. Her skin distracts me and makes me want to alter the deal. But no. It will be worth it. Monica is going to be *mine* whether she likes it or not.

"This is beautiful," she tells me.

"Thank you."

She's right, it is. I spent a lot of time on this room, working with a designer. Every choice was intentional. It's meant to initially be welcoming and disarming, but there are touches that sink in later that add intimidation. Just what you need in a room where you're trying to win poker. Dark walls and gold sconces create a shadowy atmosphere that's intimate and just a little dangerous. Red leather furnishings that are incredibly comfortable, but will also stick if you start to sweat. I love to watch people succumb to the design. It happens every time. "Make yourself comfortable." I gesture to the table in the center of the room.

She chooses the seat farthest from the door. Not uncommon. She wants to feel safer by seeing the exit, but that choice puts her further in the shadows, and when I sit down, I'm going to be between her and the door and she's going to know it.

I don't make her another drink. She has the remnants of her third whiskey. Instead, I pour a glass of water from the bar and set it in front of her. "You might need that."

She smiles at me, that mega-watt smile that I already know is fake. It's the same smile she gave the dealer right before she went all in on a hand she had a very small chance of winning. "That's the only thing I'll need. That and your checkbook."

I laugh, "Of course." I pull out a new deck of cards from the cabinet in the corner and show her that it's sealed. "So you know I'm not cheating."

"And how do you know *I'm* not cheating?" She holds up her small bag. "I could have pocket aces in here."

I raise an eyebrow. "You want to show me inside the bag then?"

She giggles, a girly sound, and I think the whiskey might be hitting her more than she realizes, but she opens the bag. There's nothing in it but a tube of lipstick and a pack of gum.

"I think I'm safe," I say.

Monica leans forward, her eyes fastened on me with serious intensity. "I don't think that. I think you're dangerous."

Sitting across from her but never breaking her gaze, I open the pack of cards. I never get tired of the feeling of fresh cards. It feels like peace and like coming home. I smile at her, intentionally letting warmth shine through. "How am I dangerous?"

"Handsome men are always dangerous," she says, leaning over the table in a way that draws my eyes to her breasts. They're very nearly spilling out of her dress, and I'd prefer them to be spilling into my hands. Maybe later I'll have the pleasure of feeling them. "They can make you want things that are bad for you."

"What sort of things? Two million dollars can't possibly be bad for you." I shuffle the cards a couple of times and set them down, then deal out chips for each of us. I give us a thousand dollars each in chips, which should be more than enough for this game.

"No, and you know that. What would be bad for me would be letting myself get distracted by that smile of yours so that you can win as easily as you think you're going to."

I raise an eyebrow. Okay. Maybe Monica is more observant than I gave her credit for. But two can play at the flirting game, and here, in the context of this, I can flirt without feeling that familiar guilt that runs through my gut whenever I think of her and the desire I hold for her. Because wooing Monica is a means to a delicious end. "I'm not the only one who has a good smile. I think people could watch your lips all night."

"Really?" she asks, blowing me a kiss.

"Really," I say, shuffling the cards again and dealing. "I've always wanted to know how your lips taste."

I see her breath catch, and her eyes darken. Perfect. She's imagining what it would be like for me to kiss her, and it's clear that she likes the idea. The only problem is that I like it too. I want to feel the way she'll yield when I tease her mouth open and take it. Own it.

Keep yourself together, Daniel.

I look at my cards, just the edges of them. Two jacks. Not the worst, not the best either. It limits my possibilities, but it's a good hand right out of the gate. No need to give away that fact. Yet. "Your bet."

Monica looks at her cards, and I can tell that she's trying to keep her face blank. But she doesn't. Not to me. Not when I've had years of reading people's smallest expressions trying to decipher everything. Her brow furrows just a tiny bit and her lips purse for a second before she manages herself. Not exactly a bad hand, but she's determined to work with it regardless.

"Call."

I nod and knock the table. I don't need to raise the bet yet. We're fine. I deal out the flop. Four, three, and queen. No help to me there, but I glance at Monica and see her brows rise just a hint, and her fingers twitch. This does help her then. Very well. She swallows, and pushes a hundred-dollar chip into the center of the table. "A hundred."

All right, she's gaining a little confidence. I smile at her. It's my best smile. The one I use when I want women to melt in front of me. And it works. She's breathing faster, looking at me. "I call you, and I raise you another hundred."

She flinches, but tosses out another chip. I'm still smiling, and she's still staring at me. "What do you really want, Monica?"

"That's not an easy question."

"What tripped you up?" I ask, grinning.

She shakes her head and takes a sip of water. "There's what I should want. And what I do want."

I burn a card and flip the turn, and I freeze my expression. The card is a jack. I now have three of a kind. That's a damn good hand and her expression tells me that it didn't help her in the slightest. "What should you want?" I ask as she knocks the table to call. I raise the bet another hundred, and she fingers her own chip.

"Why are we betting? Aren't we pretty much all in either way?"

You are, I say silently. Out loud, I say, "Of course. But betting is just as much a part of the way the game is played as the cards. I could be betting because I have the better hand. But I also could be betting to make you *think* I have better cards. But you didn't answer the question."

Monica tosses the chip into the center of the table. "I should want to win this poker hand more than anything in the world, and I do. It should be the *only* thing that I want." She looks at me involuntarily. *Interesting.*

I burn a card and flip the river. A seven. Monica sucks in a breath. So that helped her. She doesn't have a straight and she doesn't have a flush or full house. Unless she's a very good actress, I'm pretty sure that she's exactly where I want her. There shouldn't be any hand possible that can beat three of a kind.

"And what do you actually want?"

Monica fingers her chips, looking down at the table. "I want none of this to matter. I want all our history to be put aside and for us to pretend that we were two strangers that met in a casino. And to just...see what happens." Her blue eyes are dark and shining, looking up at me through her lashes. She wants me. And I let a slow smile settle across my lips. I want her too. But she doesn't realize what I already know, which is that I get what I want, and the way I want it. Even if we were two strangers who met in a casino, everything would still be on my terms. I wouldn't have it any other way.

"Maybe you'll be the rich stranger that I come across at the bar," I say. "Maybe we'll see what happens."

She peeks at her pocket cards again, and smiles. Then she pushes her chips to the center of the table. "All in. We don't have a choice anyway."

"You're right," I say, pushing my own stack in. "Let's see."

She flips over her cards, and reveals a queen and a seven. Two pair. Not bad. It could have gone her way. But it didn't.

"Your turn," she says, practically bouncing with energy.

I flip my cards, and I watch the color drain from her face

as she goes still. Then she stands up so quickly she knocks the chair over. "You cheated."

I narrow my eyes. "That's your first response? That I cheated? That's rich, coming from you, Princess." Color floods back into her face in a furious blush. "You don't know who I am sweetheart." I nod to the wall behind her near the door, the one she passed on the way in and didn't give a second look. The wall that's covered in plaques that show my poker history. Not all of them. I'd need another room for that.

Monica turns back to me, eyes blazing. "This isn't legal, you know. You can't just force me to marry you. We don't live in ancient Scotland. You can't just...carry me off and make me your bride."

I stare at her. She's incredibly beautiful when she's angry. The flush on her cheeks tells me what the color of her skin will be like when she's flushed with desire, and I want to see that pink on every inch of her skin. Even though her dress doesn't fit well—even more because of that fact— it leaves little to the imagination, and I take my time drawing my gaze down her body and back.

"You're right," I say. "We didn't have a written agreement, and I'm not going to kidnap you." She straightens, expression trending toward smug, thinking once again, that she's won. "But imagine for a second the game had gone the other way. I could easily use the same argument. It's not legal, I don't have to give you two million dollars. Do you think you would have thought our bet was legal then?"

Monica's hands ball into fists, and she grits her jaw so hard, if she were closer to me I think I'd hear her teeth crack. "So no," I say. "You don't *have* to marry me. But you will."

"Why?"

"Because if you don't, I'll tell the world that you're a liar, and a cheat, and a scammer, just like dear old daddy."

She hisses out a breath and takes a step back like I just struck her. And in a way I did. I knew that would get a reaction. Monica had nothing to do with her father's indiscretions. I know that, and she's clearly desperate to get away from that image. But the instincts are there. I can see them. Written in the lines of her face and that brilliant smile that she uses to mask and manipulate. That thing that made her stand up and call me a cheater.

She's glaring at me now, all sign of arousal and desire gone. "Fine," she spits out. "I'll marry you. You can steal my life. I'll belong to you, and you'll have the paper to prove it. But I'll never love you. I swear that you'll never have that. My heart will always be my own. You can hate me and I'll hate you. A match made in heaven."

I take a breath to calm my body down, that anger and spark making me want to cross the room, slam her against the wall and kiss her and never stop. But I get control of myself. This is perfect. Because she's given me one more weapon to use against her, and I absolutely will.

Standing, I cross the room slowly, steadily. She backs away until she's against that same wall that I wanted to push her against, and I don't stop until I'm crowding her, so close to touching her but still a breath away. "Let me make a couple things clear. First, if you call me a cheater again, there will be consequences. You won't like them. Second, I think I've made it obvious that I'm good at getting what I want. I don't need your heart, Monica."

I let her breathe for a moment, looking up at me. It's hard to ignore the way her chest is rising and falling rapidly. She's affected by my closeness even if she doesn't want to be.

"I don't need your heart," I say again, "but I'll have it. But not just that. I'll take your mind, your soul, and your body too. You're going to give them to me. You're going to *beg* me to take them."

"Never." The word is low and fervent, even as she leans closer, her body begging me to kiss her.

"We'll see," I say. And I smile.

## 4

# MONICA

This can't be happening to me. Really? Is it?

I lost. I really didn't think I would. I mean, I know that two pair isn't the best hand in poker, but no way did I think he would have three of a kind with all those bullshit cards! I had convinced myself...

I don't know. Maybe I let the whiskey get in the way of my brain. Maybe I let how sexy he was distract me. Maybe the universe can go fuck itself for not giving me a single beginner's luck win. Or maybe—and this is the truth, even if I don't want it to be—he played me. I had no idea that he had made this fortune by being amazing at poker. Though the evidence was right there for me to see when I entered the room, I just didn't notice.

How exactly did I think that he just happened to luck into owning Brazen Casinos? The money to start this place had to come from somewhere. And he probably knew that I wouldn't overthink it, because up until recently, money was just readily available to me, I never had to question where it was coming from. But he did.

Funny, really. It's the rags to riches story in reverse. I

went from having everything to nothing. And he went from nothing to everything. I can't ignore the relief I feel, even if I *hate* it. There are worse fates than marrying a man whose worth is likely in the billions. Even if he wants to tear me apart. All I know is that I won't be sleeping on the street in a week, and that feels good. Like a weight has been lifted off my shoulders, even if I would much rather have walked out of here with two million dollars.

But just like the last few years of my life, I'll deal with it.

I'm sitting now in the penthouse suite of this building. It's Daniel's private suite, and it's fucking glorious. The windows overlook the sparkling city, and the couch I'm sitting on easily costs more than some people's yearly salary. Just like the poker room downstairs, it's tasteful and luxurious. It reminds me a lot of what my family's holdings used to look like when I was younger. Back when we spent money like it was water and didn't care about the waste of it.

He told me to wait here, and I have. There are two guards here with me, silently watching. One is the man who was guarding the poker room—I heard Daniel call him Devon. And I don't know the other one. Both of them are easily twice my size, and I'd be stupid to try to get out of here with them in the way.

Regardless, Daniel made a point of telling me that. "Stay here, and don't leave," he said. "If you do, there will be a scene, and I know how much you don't like to make a scene."

The words slice through me, one more dig at our shared history and things that I can't take back even though I wish that I could. But I'm not going to run. He knows it, and I know it. After all, I don't have anywhere to go.

But he has to be joking, right? An elaborate prank as part of his plan to take revenge. Because my mind can't wrap itself around the fact that he would actually want to marry me. It just seems like too much, to tie yourself forever to someone you loathe.

*But it doesn't have to be forever*, my mind whispers. And I think that's the part that scares me. I don't know what his plans are, only that he has some. And he could take me, humiliate me, and divorce me, as with not much more than a thought. But if that happens, I'll deal with it too.

Marry Daniel Argent. I'm still tipsy from the drinks, and I let myself lean back on the couch and surrender to the images that my mind is creating. I see myself in a white dress, walking toward him down an aisle and my stomach fluttering with nerves. But then he's kissing me, and God I want to kiss that mouth. I want to feel him kiss me.

My mind spins it forward until we're more than kissing. Until we're tangled up in each other, breathless and panting and pleasured. Everything that I said I shouldn't want during that poker game, just two strangers seeking an experience with the other. Everything that I still crave. Because the way that he looks at me makes me want him, even though I know he's using it against me. I'm drunk enough and tired enough that I don't care. Let him use me. Take me. Just make me feel something other than this.

The door opens and Daniel strides in. I'm yanked out of my erotic fantasy about him, and faced with the reality. That he's here and just as fucking hot as everything that I imagined. I feel the blush rise to my cheeks, and he notices. Apparently he notices everything.

"You look flustered."

"I'm not," I say quickly.

He just chuckles and nods to his security. They leave silently, almost like they were never there at all. "You're a terrible liar."

"Why do you think I'm lying?"

He smiles, slow and sexy. "Because your body is telling a different story. About being flustered."

"*Fine*," I say. "I am. And it's because of you. Why shouldn't I be flustered in a situation where I'm going to marry a man who hates me."

"I never said I hated you."

Anger floods me. "You did."

"Past tense. I used to hate you."

Frustration and confusion are swirling in my brain, and I'm not quite sober enough for this. "But you said that you want to destroy me."

He smiles again, this time showing that dangerous, sharp side. "I want that too. I can want more than one thing at a time. And right now, I like being the one that makes you flustered, because you're sexy when you blush."

Of course, that just makes me blush more. And then he shrugs off his suit jacket, which honestly doesn't help matters. Daniel is *built*. The last time I saw him he was skinny, though old, bitchy me would have called him scrawny. The crisp white dress shirt he's wearing has been tailored just for him. Not an inch of extra fabric anywhere, showing off a trim waist and a powerful chest. It makes me wonder what he looks like working out, and the thought of him doing shirtless chin-ups makes me feel faint.

I follow the line of his arms down to his hands. Gorgeous, deft hands that I couldn't keep my eyes off of during the game. God, what I imagine those hands could do to me. I'm aching just thinking about it, and he fucking knows it too.

He crosses the distance between us, standing over me, and his eyes are burning with fire and lust. I'm not the only one imagining what it would be like for us to be together.

There's a saying about hate and passion being two sides of the same coin, and I definitely feel that right now. I hate this man. Hate what he's doing to me. And I want to strip him naked and lick every inch of his body.

I need to get a hold of myself.

"Are you comfortable?"

The question throws me off guard, because it's soft. His tone seems...almost normal, and it doesn't reflect the heat in his eyes that I can practically feel spilling over onto my skin. "What?"

"Do you have everything you need? Do I need to send people to your room to get your things?"

I shake my head. "I don't have a room here."

"Your car then?"

Taking a deep breath, I swallow. "No car. I sold it."

Daniel's eyebrows rise into his hairline. "What?"

"You guessed I needed money, and you were right. But you didn't know how much. I'm broke. That money that I lost on poker was my last, desperate attempt. I have nothing." No sense in not being honest now. "I suppose I should thank you for wanting revenge on me. You may have saved my life. I lost my apartment at the end of the week. I would have been in a shelter."

"And I imagine you have debt racked up, credit cards that Daddy used to pay off?" The words are swift and decisive and take my breath away.

I stand, nearly bumping against him. "You think you know so much, don't you Daniel Argent. Fine, judge me all you like. You don't know me. You *never* knew me, even though everyone knew you wanted to. Little poor boy who wanted to fuck the rich girl." I want the words to sting. I want him to remember what it was like when I tore him down and pushed him to the ground. I want to see fire in his eyes.

And I do see that fire. A flare of interest and pleasure that I'm fighting back.

"You know," he says, "when you used to talk to me that way, you were taller than me. Things have changed a bit." He towers over me now. "You also used to be powerful. And conceited. Guess you haven't gotten over the conceited thing yet, have you, if telling you the truth makes you that angry."

I lash out to strike him, to wipe that cruel grin off his face, and he catches my wrist before I can make contact, backs me against the nearby window. His body is pressed up against mine and *oh my God* he feels good. The strength in him holding my wrist shows me just how much he's holding back. His entire body is potential power, nothing making it more obvious than how hard he is.

I want him. I can't deny that, and neither can my body, dampening beneath my dress and my nipples tightening against his chest. His knee slips between my legs, throwing me off balance, and he presses me harder against the glass. I can't breathe, but I don't need to as long as I can feel all of him like this.

"You're not behaving as a good wife should, Monica," he whispers, lips brushing my cheek. Goosebumps run across my skin. God, I hate this man so much and I need him so much I can't remember my own name.

"That's because I'm not your wife." I say, voice raw.

"That's right. You're not. We'll get the paperwork tomorrow. And then you can decide what you want."

I shake my head again, because he's smiling at me as if he hadn't just trapped me in a corner. He still has my wrist caught in an almost bruising pressure. "What I want?"

"For the wedding. You usually only get the one, so if you

want the huge deal, Princess, we'll do that. Whatever your dream wedding is, you'll get to have that."

Confusion fizzles in my brain, added to by his closeness and the alcohol. "Why would you do that?"

Daniel releases my wrist, drawing his fingers down my arm and down the side of my back where my skin is exposed, and I shudder. "Did you think I was going to marry you and keep you in a cage? Or make you eat bread and water? No. I'm not that kind of monster. And right now, I like the idea of making you love me. So you can have whatever you want, Princess, if that's the kind of life that you want to go back to."

There's a catch. There's always a catch. He's not showing his hand, I know that, but the idea of slipping back into luxury is undeniably appealing. Even if there is an inevitable catch.

"I want to kiss you," Daniel says. The words are soft like velvet, and his fingers are still moving on my skin. Up and down, hypnotizing. So slowly, sending tingles up my spine. "And you haven't pulled away yet."

"Well? What's stopping you?" I ask him. I want him to kiss me. I like that he's telling me what he wants. That it sets up the clear expectation, since our history is complicated and everything about it is vague.

"I told you downstairs that you're going to beg me. Not for money, not for the quality of life that I expect my wife to enjoy. But for my touch, my pleasure, and my love? You'll beg. You need to earn that. I won't kiss you unless you ask me to, Princess."

Anger and desire twist up in equal measure inside me. I hate that he wants me to do that, reducing me to someone who needs to beg. But God, it makes me want to. I imagine getting on my knees and begging for more. The thought is too much, I have to close my eyes. My face flushes again, and I know that he'll notice. Know that I want him.

But I'm not going to beg this man for anything. I'm already losing too much. Already at his mercy. He won't see me do it.

However, that doesn't mean that I can't get what I want. I say nothing, just arch myself into Daniel's body and lift my lips to his. Our kiss explodes, like gunpowder and a match. His mouth consumes mine, heat and pleasure flowing through me. I groan into his mouth, and he teases my lips open with his tongue. Invading, battling, conquering mine with precision and ease.

He presses me harder against the glass, the coolness of it on my back contrasting against his heat. He's like a flame pressed against me and I want to burn. I ache everywhere for him, and his hands roam, leaving shivers in their wake. There's no hesitation in his exploration, only confidence and assurance that he already owns me—because he does. I hate that that thought makes me wet.

Daniel's hands slide up my body until they reach my shoulders, and he grabs the sleeves of my dress where they curve over my shoulders and peels it down. I don't even try to stop him. Don't want him to stop. He lets it fall so it pools around my feet and I'm in nothing but my lingerie and my one pair of high heels.

The way his eyes rove up and down my body makes me feel like his mouth is already on me, and I'm so wet that he might be able to see it. He pulls me hard against his body again, taking me with him as we sprawl down onto the couch. Instantly he's over me, delicious weight pinning me to the cushions as he plunders my mouth again. *Yes.*

This is what I wanted. Nothing but mindless pleasure and distraction. He feels so good, heat burning through the thin fabric of his shirt and hard cock pressing against me through his pants. His tongue strokes into my mouth, making me see stars behind my eyes. *More* is the only word that I can remember.

Then his lips are gone and he's breathing as hard as I am, kissing down my chest and lower. Down across my stomach, where he hovers. He could go anywhere from here. "Don't think that I didn't notice your little loophole, Princess. Make no mistake, I will have you beg. But just this once, I'll give you a pass. But only if you tell me what you want."

What do I want? I want everything. I want him to take control and take me and let us fall into a haze of pleasure together. I want to forget that he's Daniel and that I'm Monica just for the night. I want him to use me the way he wants. But his lips curl up into a smile, and I know that I have to choose. At least for now. I have every confidence that I can get him to do more. It barely took a whisper of a kiss to land us here.

"Your mouth," I say, my own mouth dry. "I want your mouth on me."

He grins, and presses a slow kiss just below my belly button. "As you wish, Princess." The words vibrate across my skin, leaving goosebumps in their wake.

Daniel licks me, dragging his tongue downward to the edge of my panties and hovering, teasing me with mouth and fingers before pulling them down. I'm already soaking wet and the sudden rush of air is cold on my pussy. But before long, it's replaced by the warmth of Daniel's mouth.

He presses a kiss to my clit, lips closed and utterly chaste, which makes me laugh. I don't know if I can actually consider a kiss on my clit *chaste*. But he kisses it gently, slowly. It's not what I want.

I want him to devour me.

Lifting my hips, I try to ask for more, but he pushes them down again, and I moan.

"I said you could ask for what you wanted. I didn't say you could tell me how to give it to you." His voice isn't angry, just firm. Utterly confident, and I grow even more wet. Of course he notices, and his chuckle makes me flush with embarrassment.

A small lick across my slit, and he makes a sound of pleasure. "You taste good, Princess. I've always wondered what this pussy tasted like. When we were younger I thought it might taste like hope, dreams, and money." Another lick, longer and slower. "But it tastes like candy to me now."

His slow exploration has me shaking. God, yes. He starts slow, light touches and flicks of his tongue. I never know where he's going to land next. My clit, my entrance, the inside of my thigh. Not knowing where the next touch will be heightens all of my senses at once.

Then the lightest of kisses on my skin, slowly pressing forward to full contact. And then a little more. Slow, solid strokes of his tongue around my clit, and I moan. It feels so good, pleasure pooling in my gut and fizzing in my veins. I relax into it, letting go of everything else. It's been so long since I had anything else to do but wonder about survival. So long since I had anybody that wanted to touch me. Taste me.

Daniel slides his hands under my ass, pulling me closer, and he doesn't hold back now. He covers my pussy with his mouth and sucks deep, before plunging in with his tongue and I cry out. Desire and delicious pleasure flare up like a flash, and I want more of this. More of all of it. I've never had anyone do this to me—have me on the edge, so close without going over and so fast.

He gives me what I want then, devouring me with lips and tongue and the occasional scrape of his teeth to make me shiver. Again and again, fucking me with his tongue until I'm moaning, unable to hold it back. I'm so close to bliss, I can almost taste it, and I'm writhing under his mouth even though his hands hold me in place.

Daniel slides upwards, stroking under my clit in a rhythm too fast for my body not to react. It does, rushing toward my orgasm like a lit fuse, and he doesn't stop. Over and over and over. And I explode like a nova. Light flashes behind my eyes as I come, pleasure lighting me up from the inside. I'm shaking, and Daniel seals his mouth over me, sucking, drinking me in. Making the pleasure last and more pleasure rise up on top of it.

The orgasm soars up and out and pleasure is spinning in me so fast that for a moment I feel weightless before crashing back to earth. Breathless, panting, spent.

Daniel's tongue is still moving on me, sending little sparks of pleasure through me. When he releases me, he crawls back up my body, planting wet kisses on my skin until he reaches my mouth and kisses me. I taste myself on his lips.

He kisses me deep. Possessive. And I want it all again. I thought that orgasm would satisfy me, but it didn't. All it did was pour fuel on a flame. I want all of him. I want him inside me. "Fuck me," I say against his lips.

Daniel's laugh is deep and dark. "I don't think so."

"What?"

He shakes his head. "I'm not going to fuck you until you're my wife."

My mind goes blank with shock, and I realize that I've

walked into a trap. Because now I *want* that. I want to fuck him, and in order to do that I have to go through with marrying him. One more assurance by him that he has me right where he wants me. It's so well played that I'm almost impressed. But two can play. I press my breasts up into his chest, reach out and stroke my hands down his sides. "You don't want to fuck me?"

I watch as his eyes go dark with lust and something else darker. "It has nothing to do with what I want," Daniel says.

"I'll beg you." I make the offer because I'm desperate and I want to see him relent for the one thing he's asked me to do. But all he does is smile slowly and shake his head. "No. I gave you a choice, and you made it. That's the end of it."

My breath goes short. "So you would have fucked me if I had asked?"

Lifting himself off me, he stands and sits in a chair across from me. "You'll never know," he says. "But if you're really that horny, you can still make yourself useful."

He doesn't make a move, but I know what he's talking about. My eyes drop to where his cock is tenting his pants. I felt him against me just moments ago, hard and hot, and despite myself, my mouth starts to water. But I'm not going to give him the satisfaction of just doing what he wants without him asking. "I'm afraid you'll have to be more specific."

He raises an eyebrow. We both know we're playing a game. "Show me how much you want to be a good wife," he says. "And do what any loving wife would do for her husband after a long day."

"I've never been married. I don't know what a loving wife would do."

That feral smile appears again. "She would crawl to me and sit at my feet. Naked."

I find myself reaching to take off my bra—the only thing left on me—and sinking to my knees on the floor. I hate this. I hate every second and the flush on my face tells him that. But I have to do it. I *have* to and I want to more than anything. I can barely comprehend the two emotions that exist side by side.

I crawl to him, watching his eyes light up watching me. He leans forward when I'm between his legs, taking my mouth in a kiss that blinds me with its passion. He's making me want him, and I know that.

It doesn't stop me from wanting him so much that I ache between my legs.

"What would she do now?" I ask breathlessly when he pulls away.

"She would undo my belt and pants, so I could be free after being restricted all day."

Rising up on my knees, I do just that. I release his belt, which is black leather, and the highest quality. And I unbutton and unzip his pants. His cock is only just hidden by tight boxer briefs, straining against the fabric. I pull it down, and it springs free. Hard. And giant.

Daniel's cock is just like the rest of him—perfectly sculpted and powerful. God, as good as that orgasm was, now I wish that I'd asked him to fuck me. He's huge and thick and would have filled me up and then some. Cocks aren't attractive, but this one is.

"And now?" I ask, my voice quiet. I know what he's going to say, but I need to hear him say it.

"She would suck his cock until he came, and swallow every bit. Hoping that afterward he'd want to fuck her."

I look up at him, and the corner of his mouth tips up into a smile. God, I hope so. I want to feel him inside me. I want to be taken by him. I can't stop staring, his dark eyes see all of me. It's not a sensation that I'm used to.

"Suck my cock, Princess."

I do.

I use just my tongue first, reaching out to touch him. He's filled with furious heat, and he feels good under me. I lick all the way up to his tip, teasing, when his hand finds my hair. His fingers grab it, tangle in it, guiding me onto him. And down, and down until my mouth is full and I can't take more before he's in my throat.

Suddenly his lips are at my ear. "I told you to *suck*." He pulls me up off his cock and holds me close. "Do I need to show you exactly what I expect from you? *Wife?*"

We're still playing the game. Still in this hypothetical scenario, and I want it. I don't want to break free of it. "Yes. Show me how to be a good wife," I say.

The words are barely out of my mouth before he's driving me back onto his cock. All the way down, slipping into my throat and further so my lips are pressed against his skin. Deeper than I thought possible. God, I love it.

His hand holds me in place, not forcing, just holding. Keeping me where he wants to. His voice is a low growl when he speaks. "A good wife takes all of her husband's cock."

Daniel pumps his hips into my mouth, and I groan around him. I'm so wet that I'm dripping down my thighs. Never in my life did I think a blowjob could turn me on like this, but I love the feeling of him, of taking him completely.

He pulls back and lets me breathe before guiding me down again, this time I'm moving before he makes me. I suck my way down, taking him completely and he groans, fingers tightening in my hair. His other hand joins the first, securing me in place. "Now stay there."

He fucks my mouth, my throat, pumping deep, and I

can't escape. I don't want to. Everything else fades away and it's just me and him in the moment. Daniel grunts with each thrust, and it doesn't take him long before he groans, cock swelling in my mouth. He's so far down my throat that I don't even have to swallow.

Daniel holds me still until he's finished, until I'm dizzy from lack of air, and the world comes flying back when he releases me. I'm panting, trying to gather myself. Cause clearly, I've gone a little crazy.

I look up at Daniel, and he's staring at me, and I can't decipher his expression. It's hard and gentle at once. But his eyes are filled with that fire that I can't fight against.

"Again," he says.

"What?" My voice is rough.

"Now that I've shown you what I expect, suck my cock. Again. You need to earn the taste of my cum this time, Monica."

The use of my name startles me. It's easy to pretend that this isn't me when he calls me *princess* and *wife*. But this is *me*. And I don't understand why I want this. But I do.

So I lower my head and take him into my mouth again.

5

———

**DANIEL**

The sight of Monica on her knees in front of me is better than I ever imagined—and I have imagined it a *lot*. The way her lips stretch around my cock The way she takes all of me with ease...God, I'm lucky that I lasted as long as I did the first time around.

I love being in control, and she likes it, too, even if she doesn't want to admit it. I saw the confusion in her eyes just now when I ordered her to suck me, but she did it anyway. She doesn't understand why she's doing it, but she knows she's driven to.

I'm a bastard—I'll admit that. I took advantage of her situation for my own ends, and I don't regret it. But I'd never actually force her. I know her needs better than she does, though. And she needs this marriage more than she's willing to let on. I'll bet that no one in her life has given her any kind of boundaries or direction. I'm happy to be the first.

I like that soft look on her face of confusion and desire, and fuck, I love the way her pussy tastes. But I will control myself, and she needs to know that I'm serious. I'm not going to fuck her until the papers are signed, and even then, not until she begs for it.

What I'll never admit is that right now, my control is wavering. I'm teetering on the edge of giving her whatever she wants. Thankfully she can't read my mind.

Monica is sucking my cock enthusiastically, and it's so fucking good. She dips back down and takes me into her throat again, bobbing up and down and moaning. I feel like a teenager because I could probably come again right now. But I won't. I didn't lie. She needs to earn it. She needs to show that she can follow through and get a reward.

Up and down she goes, sucking the tip of me and using her tongue under my head in a way that makes my toes curl inside my shoes. And down, until her face is entirely hidden by her hair and her bottom lip is brushing my balls.

I'm not going to be able to last as long as I'd like. She has me too turned on and I want her too badly to hold myself back forever. She's too busy to notice that my knuckles are white holding on to the arms of the chair. Pleasure is building in my balls and around my shaft, making me close my eyes. It hums, and every stroke of her lips and tongue amplifies it. *Yes.*

I let myself fade into the rhythm of her mouth, floating through the fog of pleasure until it rears up, and I'm so close that I can't breathe. I grasp her hair again, and pull her off me, tilting her head back so I can see her face. "Open your mouth," I tell her, standing up. My cock is still resting on her lips, and I hold her exactly where I want her while I stroke myself, finding that pleasure that sends me over the edge.

Monica opens her mouth, and I groan, my cum splashing across her tongue. Stream after stream of it pooling in her mouth. She doesn't flinch or hesitate, taking all of it until I'm finished. And it's the hottest fucking thing I've seen in my life.

"Swallow," I say, and she does. The look on her face is priceless. She closes her eyes and it looks like she savors the taste of me on the way down. When she opens her eyes again, she licks the tip of my cock, and I'm ready to get down on my knees and give her whatever the fuck that she wants for the rest of her life. But that's not what she needs, and the hope and desire I see in her eyes right now needs to be taken care of. Even if it's not the way she wants.

"I think you have a chance of being a good wife, Princess."

She smiles before she catches herself. "And does my husband want to fuck me now?"

Putting my cock away, I pull her to her feet and guide her to the guest room. She's still naked, and I retrieve a robe from the bathroom and wrap it around her. She looks confused again, so I tilt her face up to meet mine. "I made myself clear," I say. "I'm not fucking you until we're married. And even then, you know the rules."

Her happiness crashes. I can see it. "I'll have to beg."

"Yes."

"Why?" The word is small and sad, and I feel a flinch inside. I don't want to hurt her. "You hate me that much?"

I take her by the hair again and force her eyes to mine. I like having my hand in her hair. It's soft and silky against my skin, and the way her breath catches when I tighten my fingers in it makes me hard. And I like that I can make her do what I like when I have her like this. She likes it too. "I already told you that I don't hate you. But no matter what money troubles you've had, Princess, everything has come easy to you. You don't know what it's like to have to ask for something and be told no, and have to accept that."

"You don't know that," she says viciously. "You have no idea what my life has been like."

"And I'm going to hear it. But you are mine. You are marrying me. And I want you to learn what it's like to ask for the things you want. Right now, I know that the thing that you want is me. So you can feel free to ask me any time. Beg me *any time*. Sometimes I'll say yes, and sometimes I'll say no."

"But—"

"But nothing. You need boundaries, Monica, and you'll learn them with me."

She tries to pull away from me, but I don't let her go. I wrap my arm around her waist and hold her naked body pinned against me. She'll feel how turned on I am already, and I don't care. I love the way she feels.

"Fuck you," she spits out.

"You wish," I say simply, smiling, and I'm rewarded with a glare that would level me if looks could kill. And then I kiss her. Her body reacts first, going limp and pliant against me. I know the moment she realizes what's happening and goes still. So I release her, stepping back. I meant it when I said I wouldn't force her. But I know that I won't have to.

"For the few days until we're married," I say, "this will be your room. I'll have some pajamas delivered from downstairs, and feel free to call for room service. But know that Devon and Jack are outside."

"So no running away."

She has no idea how sexy she looks, robe gaping and showing a delicious glimpse of her cleavage. "We both know that you don't want to run, though you can keep pretending if you like."

The blush on her face is lovely.

"I'll make sure you have clothes in the morning, and we can make other arrangements. Goodnight, Monica."

I close the door behind me as I exit the guest bedroom. She's not locked in, and I'm sure she'll test that, but she won't see me again tonight. She needs space now to figure out her own thoughts without me clouding them. It will be interesting to see how she feels in the morning. I'm really good at reading people, but Monica Blast is unpredictable. It could go either direction. She could suddenly decide to behave, or not. I think it'll be somewhere in between.

She doesn't want this, but she needs it. I need it too, and that's the thing that I don't want to admit. I say that I'm doing this for revenge, and I am. But it's not just that. I won't allow myself to let the thought raise about why I'm really doing it.

Seems like Monica isn't the only one who needs time to get her thoughts sorted. I pour myself a drink. I rarely have more than two in a night, but I'm done. I'm not going downstairs again—everything is taken care of on that front—and all I'm going to do is relax and sleep.

Just hours ago I thought that I needed a good fuck to relax. Never imagined that this would happen. It wasn't a fuck, but I wouldn't have it any other way. I think that I was wrong when I was thinking that I need a vacation. The truth is that I've never really known what to do on vacations. My entire life I've had to work, and taking pure leisure time, even when I can afford to do it, feels strange.

What I actually needed was a project, and I found one. Monica. I feel more refreshed than I have in ages, and it's not because she sucks cock better than any woman I've ever been with. I'm excited about this. About learning about her. About teaching her. And yes, about making her pay for what she's done. I'll always admit that I'm a bastard—I am.

I'm going to enjoy pleasuring her as much as all the rest of it.

But after everything she and her family have done to me, I need closure. And I'm going to have it.

I take out my phone and browse the boutiques downstairs, finding some sexy lingerie and nightgowns that I order and make sure it's expedited. The clothes should be delivered to the room within fifteen minutes. I intentionally choose things that are sexy and that will remind Monica of everything that we are not doing in my bed right now. I wanted to infiltrate her brain, to the point where she can't resist sliding her hands into her panties thinking about it.

To be honest, I don't want her to touch herself without me there to watch. Perhaps I'll suggest that tomorrow when she asks again. Because she will ask again. And I'm not sure if I'm strong enough to say no, even if I need to be.

Taking my drink, I step out onto the balcony for some fresh air. The Las Vegas air is warm tonight, which isn't uncommon. But tonight it also feels refreshing to me. I'm not used to this level of obsession in my thoughts. A new project is good, something that's going to throw me off my game is not.

I shouldn't care if Monica is happy, but I do. I shouldn't care if she is comfortable, but all I want to do is go back inside and make sure that she's taken a shower and is wrapped in the most comfortable robe and pajamas that I can get my hands on. I want to lay her on her back and explore her body far more thoroughly than I had the chance to tonight. The way she tastes, I want to lick her skin. I want to taste every inch of her. I want her to beg me to explore her with my mouth. I want to spend the whole night making her writhe in pleasure, but never letting her come.

As I look out over the city, I find myself thinking of ways

that I can make her happy. Things that we can do together that will make her feel better about what's happened to her. The thought startles me. I shouldn't care about that. I can feel my decades old desire for her creeping back in. I can feel it making me soft.

In that space, there's suddenly anger. Deep, dark, and furious. I got over this years ago. I need to hate her, even if I told her that I didn't. She was my tormentor. She bullied me. Her family shattered mine, and nearly annihilated it. It doesn't matter that our situations are reversed now, nothing can make up for that. Ever.

But all I can think about right now is her lips. How soft they were. How she tasted, and how she sounded in her pleasure. And beyond that, the sheer and utter desperation in her eyes when she lost her hand. She was right when she told me that I did not know what she has gone through. I don't. But I will.

In the end it doesn't matter. There is a debt that is owed between us, and she will be the one to pay it. I don't know how yet, but I'll figure it out. After all, we have the rest of our lives to figure it out. I have a plan.

I'm going to break her down.

I'm going to make her pay her debt.

And then I'm going to make her love me.

And in my mind, though I can't fully admit to myself yet, I know that after that, I'm going to make her mine forever.

Monica's desperation and fear flash into my head again, and I feel something that I haven't felt in a very long time. Empathy. I know exactly what she was feeling in those moments, because I felt it too. For the second time this evening, I feel myself swept away in the grip of memory.

I was seventeen the last time that I saw Monica. I was working at the auto repair shop where I spent most of my time finishing school, and where my obsession with poker first began. I was running myself ragged, trying to keep my grades up in school while working a full-time job. We had already lost our house to the Blast Dynasty at that point. It was up to me to make rent on the tiny apartment that my parents and I were living in, or else we would be once again living in our car. All three of us.

Which would have meant that I would end up sleeping in the park, likely on a bench. The weather was nice that time of year, so it wouldn't have been entirely unpleasant, but I had already been discovered sleeping outside by one too many classmates for me to want to do that again. So I made it work. I fit in my homework in the down times at the garage, coming in early to work hours before school, cleaning and organizing, and pulling the late shifts afterwards so I could have as many hours as possible.

I will always be grateful to the owner of that garage. He was always understanding, and willing to give me the hours I needed because he knew what was happening. He was incredibly gracious with letting me work on my homework while on shift, though he was never a person who let me slack off on the job.

The day that I last saw her I was getting ready to leave the shop. I had a project due in my biology class the next day, and I hadn't even started it. The entire garage was clean, and I was the last one there. Technically, we were already closed. I heard a screeching sound behind me, and a BMW came reeling into the garage way too fast. I had to jump to get out of the way.

The car was full of laughing teenagers from my school. I recognized them as the popular kids, the rich ones. They were the kids that hung out with Monica. The cool kids club that nobody else was allowed to be a part of. And it was incredibly clear that they were drunk. The guy in the passenger seat was laughing the hardest and shoving at the driver.

It was then that I realized the driver was Monica. I hated her then. I hated her for what her family had done to me, and I hated her because I wanted her so much. When I saw her, she looked panicked. She wasn't drunk, but she wasn't laughing either.

I didn't want to talk to them. I wanted to send them away because we were already closed, and I knew that whatever they would ask would take me away from my schoolwork. But at the same time, I knew that if I didn't talk to them that my life would get harder than it already was. So purely out of self-preservation, I walked over to them.

I should have known that as soon as they saw me the harassment would start. It had been open season on me for all the rich kids since the day that Monica threw my Game Boy in the street. I was known as a liar, thief, and all around poor trash. The idea that I might work for a living was offensive to them. Even more so after we lost our house and it was discovered that we were homeless for a while. Not being as well-off as them was the worst possible fate. Never mind that they didn't understand hardship, or had suffered anything for a day in their lives. For them, it was enough to warrant my regular public humiliation.

I ignored the insults that they were yelling at me, and ignored their laughter. I let it roll off me like I did every day at school. I was used to it. This was no different

Monica got out of the car as I walked over, and it was the first time I remember ever seeing her nervous. But all the same, when her friends cheered her on, she smiled, flipped her hair over her shoulder, and looked at me like a bug that she was ready to squash.

"I need my oil changed and my tires rotated," she said.

"You do realize that we're closed, right?"

"I know," she said. "But I'm hoping you'll do it anyway."

"I don't have a reason to do that."

She looks nervous again. "Please? I was supposed to do it earlier because my dad asked me to but didn't get around to it because they made me drive around to all these parties."

Only rich kids partied on a Sunday. Only people with the luxury of not having to work at all, even on the weekday, would consider going on a drinking spree the day before school. I don't know what possibly possessed me to say what came out of my mouth next, but I did. "It'll take me some time. I'm the only one here, everyone else has left for the day."

She looked incredibly relieved, and I felt my heart start to race in spite of myself. She looked beautiful that day, in a white dress, brown hair gently curling around her shoulders. Even though it had gotten me into trouble before, I couldn't help but imagine myself leaning forward to kiss her. It was what I had always wanted to do, inexplicably. Because how could I have this kind of desire for someone so shallow? For someone who had no regard for others? But as I had discovered many times in my life, the heart wants what it wants and there's nothing that you can do to stop it.

"Thank you."

Brakes squealed from the other side of the garage, and a new car skidded to a stop. Instantly there was a guy I recognized as Monica's boyfriend stepping out of the driver seat and calling her name. "Monica, let's go. The next party awaits!"

He was obviously more drunk than the rest of them. To the point where he couldn't even pretend that he was safe to drive, but he was doing it anyway. I remember feeling a burning anger sizzling through my veins, and the desire to put him in his place. To put them all in their place.

Monica looked at me. "I'll be back later for the car."

"Hurry up, Mon!"

Up until this point, I'd always stayed silent. It's how I'd survived. But I couldn't watch her get into that car and say nothing. And a smaller part of me hoped that she would say yes, and stay with me. "You don't have to go with him."

Her face suddenly changed, going slack with shock. For a moment, just a moment, I thought that she was going to change her mind. But then the guy was beside her, gripping her arm with a nearly bruising force and pulling her toward the car. "Let's go. Now."

I took a step forward. "She can make her own decisions. And you are way too drunk to drive, so back off."

The guy started to laugh, the kind of laugh that only drunk people have going for them. "Who the fuck are *you*, man? Just fix the goddamn car and stop talking to my girlfriend."

I didn't respond to him. I only looked at Monica. "You're welcome to stay here while I fix the car. I'll make sure you get home."

She still looked shocked and surprised, and it's the last thing I saw before I went flying. The boyfriend had come at me and I hadn't even seen it. His intoxicated state hadn't altered his speed at all, and he shoved me backwards into the wall of tools. I didn't even know that until later. All I knew in that moment was pain. My head had cracked against the wall, and all I could see was red.

I opened my eyes to Monica's horrified face. It's the face I remember most. All she did was stare at me. Even as her friends dragged her into the car, and pulled out so quickly that they left black tire marks on the floor, all she did was stare.

The reason I remember so clearly was because it was the first time I had ever seen Monica Blast show her humanity.

Eventually, after a while, I picked myself up off the floor. I had bruises for a week from flying into the wall. But I fixed the car. The entire time I was doing it, I thought about Monica. I hoped that she would be okay, and that her asshole of the boyfriend wouldn't get in an accident and kill her. Or that the way he grabbed her arm didn't extend to the rest of their relationship and was just because he was drunk. I remember thinking that it wasn't any of my business. I remember being angry that it was her fault I was working so late, even though I had agreed to it. I remember being angry because of the unfairness of it all.

But mostly I remember just hoping that she would be okay.

I never spoke to Monica Blast again after that day. I saw her a few times at school, but it wasn't long after that that I had to drop out of school entirely in order to make ends meet.

If the boy in that garage had known where he would end up, and where Monica would end up, he wouldn't have believed it. I still don't believe it. But now she's here, and she is certainly not okay.

The coin is still in the air about whether she will be after I'm through with her. No matter how I feel about her, there's still a debt to pay.

## 6

## MONICA

When I wake up, my memory is hazy. I remember that I was at the casino last night, but not much else. I am in a bed that is not my apartment, and the sheets that are over me probably cost more than my rent. I haven't been poor enough to forget the feeling of thousand thread count sheets. When I look at what I'm wearing, the lingerie—a sky blue baby doll nightgown trimmed in silver lace— is equally as expensive.

I sit up, and look around. Holy shit, where am I?

This is one of the nicest hotel suites I've ever been in, and I've been in my fair share of the nice hotels. The carpet is plush when my feet hit the ground, and I quickly open the curtains to the morning sun. The city of Las Vegas sparkles before me, so I clearly didn't go home. I've been living on the outskirts for a couple of years, because everybody needs lawyers in Las Vegas and usually they don't have qualms about the past history of their lawyers. Unless you're me.

Go figure, I would run into the one person I least expected.

With that thought, everything comes rushing back. My bad first run of poker, Daniel's appearance, my second bad run of poker and the bet that I cannot believe I actually made, and everything that came after it. The blush that rushes up my chest and face is painful as I remember what we did. I was on my knees for him, and I liked it.

I wish I could say that it was all the alcohol that I had, and my head is certainly pounding with a hangover. But even at my drunkest, I am never a person that does things she doesn't want to. Everything that happened last night came from a place that I cannot explain and don't understand.

I didn't see him after he left me last night, though the clothes he ordered appeared barely a half-hour after he disappeared. I looked for him, but he was nowhere to be found. This suite is huge though, and I remember feeling like I might get lost, so I just went to bed instead.

I sit down on the bed and run my hand over the comforter. I can't remember the last time I felt such luxury. It was truly years ago before I left my parents house for college. College was great. Granted, I'm sure my college experience was much more luxurious than other people's, but at the time, to me, it felt like slumming it.

And then after that is when it all started to disappear. The scandals and the lies were starting to unravel, and suddenly there just wasn't enough to go around anymore. It's only been the last couple of years that have been truly bad, but still, touching fabric like this brings back memories for me. I can't even say that the memories are bittersweet. I enjoyed being wealthy. People will call me shallow for admitting it, but there are huge benefits. It's nice to not have to worry about money, and these last few years, in financial panic, have really shown me how good I had it.

And have it again, apparently.

He said he was serious, but he can't be, really. People

don't make bets about marriages. That just doesn't happen. Would he really have let me walk out of his casino with $2 million? Maybe he would have. But this new Daniel doesn't seem like the kind of person that makes bets he doesn't know he is going to win. So why would he bet the marriage at all?

It's all so confusing it makes my head spin.

I remember last night he said that he would buy me clothes, but right now, I don't see any. All I have is this night-gown, the panties I'm wearing beneath it, and the gown I wore last night which is likely still on the floor of the living room. Part of me doesn't dare leave this room wearing this, and the rest of me is saying that I'm silly. After everything that happened last night, after being on my knees with his cock down my throat, it seems a little foolish to play the prude.

But still, I'm hesitant. What is he going to say when he sees me? How do I face him after that? But it's not like he doesn't know I'm in here, and it's not like I can just sit in here all day and hide. As if to get me off my ass, my stomach growls at that moment. I guess my body is telling me to stop being a chickenshit and leave the room.

The room I'm in is bigger than I remember last night. It's actually a suite, with double doors that lead into living room. I try to open one of the doors quietly, but the large door isn't quiet. In fact, the loud clicking of the lock opening seems like it's screaming into the silence just for me. Of course.

If Daniel is awake, there's no chance that he doesn't know I'm here.

I think that there was a dining room somewhere on the other side of the living room, and maybe a kitchen. But I don't have to explore much, because I can smell food cooking. It smells delicious, like eggs and pancakes. All I have to do is follow my nose.

I walk around the corner from the living room into the open dining room, and I'm proven correct—there is a huge table piled with food. Everything that I smelled along with fruit and yogurt, bacon and sausage and ham. It's a literal feast, and my stomach growls again.

Daniel is sitting at the head of the table, reading the paper. I didn't realize that people even read the paper anymore, but it looks so natural for him to be doing it that I don't doubt it's something that he does every day. He's dressed in just a jeans and t-shirt, but is no less sexy than he was in the suit. Just in a different way, more casual. Though I don't doubt that feral side of him is lurking just beneath the surface. I take a moment to drink him in, examining the way the jeans hug his thighs, and the way the t-shirt exposes the perfect physique I only got to feel last night.

He lifts a cup of coffee to his lips, and just like last night when I watched him drink the whiskey, I'm fascinated by the motion. It's so simple and so graceful, and yet it holds that restrained power that radiates from every inch of him.

He sees me standing in the doorway, and I'm suddenly aware of how little I'm wearing. His eyes take me in from head to toe, slowly. The feeling is almost visceral, like he's dragging his fingertips from my scalp down the back of my neck across my shoulders and down my ribs and thighs to my toes and all the way back up. My nipples harden beneath my nightgown, and there's no way he doesn't see it. The fabric is far too thin to hide anything.

He raises an eyebrow. "Good morning."

"Morning."

"How are you feeling?"

Awkward. Insecure. Embarrassed. Utterly unsure of

what you want from me. I don't say those things out loud, though. "Okay, I guess."

"I'm sorry that I haven't ordered you clothes yet," he says. "I wasn't sure of your sizing, and I don't know what kind of clothes you like to wear, so I figured I'd just let you choose."

"From where?"

He shrugs. "Anywhere you like. There are boutiques in the hotel— like the one I ordered from last night— that will deliver here to the suite. And you know Las Vegas is filled with stores. Most of them know who I am and will send a selection over if that's what you want."

I shake my head. "I don't understand."

Daniel grins at me, and impish grin that does strange things to my stomach. "Which part?"

"You're just going to buy me clothes?"

He looks at me again, taking in my appearance. His eyes dark, in a way that's familiar and arousing, but he doesn't make a move toward me or say anything about it. "Do you have any?"

I do. But they're not nice clothes. I sold all the nice ones. And the ones I do have are at my apartment forty miles away. So I shake my head. "No, I guess not."

"Then yes," he says. "I am buying you clothes. I can't have my wife walking around like that. Though you can feel free to walk around here like that anytime you want."

I walk over to the table and sit down in a chair close enough that I feel like we can still have a conversation, but far enough away that I don't feel that gravitational pull toward him. "So I suppose that dream I had last night where I bet that I would marry you and you won wasn't a dream?" I know it's not a dream, but I still have to ask anyway.

"No, it wasn't a dream. I have a lawyer coming here in an hour to draw up the papers."

"Okay." The conversation that we had just before he left my room last night is coming back to me, and I don't want to go over it again even though I still don't get it.

"I'm assuming you have your passport and other important documents at your apartment?"

"Yeah," I say. "Honestly, there's not much left there, but I should probably get that stuff."

Daniel stands and goes into the living room for a second. When he comes back, he's holding my purse, the one that I had completely forgotten about. He holds it up. "Are your keys in here?"

I nod.

He reaches inside and grabs the keys and then taps out a quick message on his phone. Elsewhere in the huge suite, I hear a door open. The huge bouncer that I remember from last night, guarding both the door of the poker room and me when he left me here, enters the dining room. Devon. I flush bright red in embarrassment, because I'm only wearing lingerie. But neither Daniel nor Devon seem concerned in the slightest. Devon barely glances in my direction. "Mr. Argent?" he asks.

"Monica, what's your address?" Daniel asks me as he hands Devon the keys to my apartment.

I give it to them. There's nothing there worth stealing, and Daniel has no reason to steal.

"Get a crew together, and go to the apartment. Empty it of anything left belonging to Miss Blast and have those things sent to my home. Have her important documents— passport, birth certificate, Social Security— anything like that, here within the hour."

"You got it," Devon says. And then he exits the apartment without another word.

"He's your go-to guy?" I asked.

Daniel nods. "He is one of them. I found it's not good to have just one go-to guy. If you give someone that kind of power, they are likely to abuse it."

How true that is. I remember when I was a kid, my father employed a man named Matthew. Matthew was in charge of almost everything directly below my father. Though I haven't had the guts to voice this opinion or ask the question, I deeply suspect that Matthew was the source of my father's corruption. That he saw an opportunity to make more money than he had ever dreamed of and thought nothing of the consequences of the people he was hurting.

But then again, that might just be hoping and wishing that my father isn't as terrible of a person as the rest of the world believes him to be.

I fill my plate with some of the amazing smelling food and eat. Daniel goes back to reading his newspaper like someone who stepped out of the men's fashion magazine.

So there's going to be a lawyer here. This is actually going to happen. "Are you going to have me sign a prenuptial agreement?"

Daniel looks up from where he's reading. "Do you think I need to do that?"

"As a lawyer, I would say yes. You're a man who's worth is likely in the billions of dollars. You're marrying somebody on a whim and any divorce in the future would likely immensely reduce your net worth."

"And what would you say as a woman and not a lawyer?"

"That I don't know why you're marrying me in the first place, so I wouldn't even know what to put in a prenuptial agreement. Of the two of us, you have all the assets. Of the two of us, you're the one who can choose to drop me at any time. Because of that, it is to my benefit not to sign one. In case you decide you're done with all this. Even if the split wasn't 50-50, I wouldn't be back on the street."

He nods. "That sounds fine then. No agreement it is."

"You're crazy," I say.

"That's not the first time that I've been told that in my life. You don't get to my position without people thinking that you're some kind of evil genius. Even if all it was was a combination of luck and determination."

"You're really going to risk your entire fortune on a marriage that you are going into because you won a hand of poker?"

Daniel folds the newspaper and sets it on the table. "I guess luck and determination aren't all that's required. I am very good at reading people. And I'm very good at predicting how things will turn out. I may have bet our marriage on the hand of poker, but that doesn't mean I haven't thought it through."

"So you were serious when you said you'd give me a big wedding?"

"Of course."

This could go so many directions. Weddings get expensive fast, and I wonder what it will take to realize that he's in over his head. "What about Paris?"

He nods. "I have some business associates in Paris. We're working on opening some European branches of Brazen Casinos. A wedding on top of the Eiffel Tower could be fun."

"I'll have to have at least two dresses. One for the ceremony and one for the reception. Maybe a third if there's a cocktail hour."

"I'll have my assistant pull a list of designers that I've worked with before. I'm sure some of them would be ecstatic to work with you." He takes a slow sip of his coffee, staring me down, not taking the bait.

"What about Bali?"

"The pictures in Bali would be nice. Very good for social media and the newspapers. Because naturally people are going to want to know that I got married. I'm sure you can expect a lot of people to attend the wedding. That would be my only complaint about Bali. It wouldn't exactly be conducive to a large affair."

I take a bite of pancake, pondering. "What about the Taj Mahal? It's certainly big enough."

He chuckles. "I'll see what I can do."

"And I'd like a world tour for the honeymoon. There are plenty of places that I've always wanted to see but have never gotten to."

Daniel leans back in his chair and puts his arms behind his head. "If you plan it, and as long as I have an Internet connection from which to do work, then that sounds fine."

"And of course I'll need real live monarch butterflies to be released after we say I do."

Daniels eyes narrow and he suddenly sits up. "Come here."

I freeze. "What?"

"Come here."

I don't know what's going to happen, but I get up from my chair and walk the few feet to his. Without warning, Daniel grabs my hips and pulls me onto his lap so that my knees are straddling his waist. The sudden proximity makes me catch my breath, dizzy with his presence. His hands wrap around my wrists and hold them down by my sides. "I know what you're doing, Princess. It's not going to work."

"I'm only trying to plan a fabulous wedding, husband."

"No," he says. "You're trying to push me. You're trying to go so far that I think you're more trouble than you're worth. You're trying to get me to walk away."

I blush, the now familiar feeling of embarrassment washes over me. He sees what I'm thinking three steps ahead of me. I don't say anything to him.

"I'm only going to say this one time," Daniel says. "So you better fucking listen. You can ask me for whatever you want. If you want to get married on the goddamn moon, I'll do my best to make it happen. If you want to get married at the bottom of the Mariana's Trench, I have people I can talk to. If you want to re-create the wedding scene from Moulin Rouge, that is well within the range of possibility.

"But what you will not do is get me to walk away. It's not going to fucking happen. And if you think that you, Monica Blast, can possibly scare me? Then you have absolutely no idea who you're dealing with."

The way he's looking at me, the fire and passion in his gaze, should scare me. What it shouldn't do is turn me on even though that's exactly what I'm feeling, and the way I'm straddling him, it's only going to be moments before he notices. Even if I don't have very many choices, I still have my pride.

I'm not going to let him conquer me with a few stern words. But my voice is far breathier than I like when I manage to speak. "I remember who I'm dealing with," I say. "I remember a thin and scraggly boy who never spoke up to defend himself. I remember a boy who was so afraid that he made himself an easy target. I remember that you just took anything that anybody threw at you because you weren't strong enough to fight back."

It only takes a second, and I'm on the floor. Daniel is over me, his presence overwhelming. All I can see is him. All I can feel is him, his hands on my skin where he grabbed me to bring us down here. The thin nightgown has ridden up exposing my panties and most of my stomach. I can feel the scratch of his jeans on my legs and it's all I want to feel. The cold metal of his belt buckle sends shivers across my skin along with memories of undoing it on my knees last night.

"You forget that I remember you too, Monica," he breathes in my ear. His voice is dark, suddenly riding that sharp line that shows itself when he lets go. "And you like to push people. Push and push until people did what you wanted. Even if you had no right to ask it of them. You pushed me. Literally. Figuratively. And I took it because I had more important things to deal with in my life than being your goddamn lapdog. I bet you never even noticed when I left school did you?"

He said last night that he had to drop out of school, but in the haze of seeing him again, that was a detail that I didn't remember until just now. And I hate that he's right. Until the moment he introduced himself at the bar, I hadn't thought about Daniel Argent in probably ten years. I didn't notice that he wasn't at graduation. I didn't notice that he was gone at all. "No," I whispered.

He drags his hand up my skin, starting at my knees and not losing contact until his hand is wrapped around my throat. Not squeezing. Not threatening. But to show his dominance and strength. "I am not that boy anymore," he says. "Do you want me to prove it to you? Do you want to push me until I go over the edge? Until I can't do anything else but sink my teeth into you and never let go?"

I am no longer in control of myself, and the groan that comes from me is completely involuntary. Yes. I do want that. I want his harsh, brutal, self. I want him to punish me for everything that I've done wrong. There's plenty of it, and if it's Daniel doing the punishment and not a stranger, at least I know that I deserve it.

His mouth crashes down on mine, and I'm lost. Heat and darkness and lust surge through me. God, the way he makes me feel is indescribable. I've never had anyone make me feel this way before. This raw, natural chemistry.

Hate and lust are a thin line—I've always known that. But this is the first time I'm actually experiencing it. His hand is still around my throat, the other one slowly inching down toward my pussy. I want him there. I want him there so badly that I can't breathe.

Daniel's tongue invades my mouth, reminding me of exactly what he can do with it elsewhere. I'm shamefully wet from just his kiss. I hate that he can do this to me. Capture my body with his pleasure and make it his. And at the same time, I love every single second.

His fingers slide over my panties, coming to rest right over my clit, and freeze. Nothing but the thin lace separates him from touching my skin, and I wiggle my hips to try to get him closer. He doesn't move.

"You know what to fucking do, Monica."

Oh God. My mind goes blank. He wants me to beg for it. My mind is screaming no, but my body is screaming yes. It's exactly what he wants. He moves his finger just a fraction, adding enough pressure to make me moan. "Please," I say against his lips, my voice barely a whisper. "Please touch me."

Daniel smiles with grim satisfaction. "Good girl, Princess."

He slides his hand under the fabric, and his fingers sink into my pussy with shocking ease. I'm so wet that he goes in deep, pulling another moan from me as he kisses me again. Fuck.

Pleasure shocks through me, hard and fast, and I'm ready to come in seconds. But I don't want it to be over. I'm arching up into his hand, seeking every ounce of pleasure that he's giving me. Drowning in it. I'm so close. So, so close.

Daniel tears his mouth away from mine. "You're not fucking done," he growls. "You will beg me to come."

I shudder. No. I'm not going to do that. It's right there, just out of reach, and he's not going to deny me that. I already begged him once. He's not that much of a monster. I say nothing and close my eyes, pressing my hips into his fingers.

They disappear.

My eyes fly open, and I find his hard eyes staring down at me. I growl in frustration. Fuck this, I'm not going to lose my orgasm because of him. I shove my hand between my legs, and he catches my wrist before I can even make contact. He pulls my arm over my head, and releases my throat to grab my other wrist. Suddenly, both wrists are in one of his hands, pinned above my head.

The look on his face is fury and fire and lust all at the same time, pure exasperation. The contrast would be amusing, if I weren't so desperately aware of our positions and my quickly fading pleasure. "Dammit, Daniel."

"Beg."

"No."

"Then we're done."

He smiles when I make a desperate noise of protest, not letting me go. "I don't understand," I say. "I can't. How can you promise to give me everything I want for a wedding? Clothes. Money. Trips around the world. And not give me a simple fucking orgasm?"

He leans close, and I know that he sees the way I'm trembling. It doesn't matter that I haven't come, I'm more aroused than I've ever been in my life. And he speaks words that cut me to the core.

"Because you don't actually care about the wedding. Not yet, anyway. You don't care about trips or the clothes or any of it. You enjoy it, but you don't *care* about it. Everything you've ever known has been handed to you. And you've never had to fight for the things you care about.

"Right now, I know that you care about your orgasm. It makes you feel something."

"I hate you," I say, trying to fight my way out of his grip. It doesn't faze him in the slightest. "I know," he says, "but you're still going to beg."

I thrust my chin up. "And if I don't?"

"I've got all day," he says. "I'll keep you here, and bring you to the edge over and over until you're so mindless with it that you don't have a choice."

Anger and arousal flood my system. I feel like I can't breathe. His face softens for a second, and I feel his fingers creep back down. He enters me smoothly, and I groan. It's perfect, the feeling of his fingers stroking inside, brushing that makes light flash behind my eyes. I'm on the edge again in seconds. "You've done so well, Princess. You already asked for this. Ask for more."

I shake my head. I can't give in. Not when it feels like I'm going to lose part of myself. He kisses me so tenderly that I feel a surge of emotion, confusing and beautiful and welcome. It's like he's asking me to let go and trust him. And in a way he is. Asking for what I want. "I need it."

"What do you need?"

I can't look at him, and I close my eyes. "I need to come."

His fingers speed up, pleasure rolling up through my spine and all the way to where his hand holds my wrists.

"No," he says. But before I can say anything, he covers my mouth with his. Sweet and soft and deepening. "But keep asking. That's the other thing you've never heard,

Monica. The word no. So you're going to keep asking until I decide that you've had enough. Fight me all you want, but I'm going to win. I'm going to own you, Princess. Heart and soul."

His fingers work me in sure strokes, thrusting against my G-spot and making fireworks explode in my core. I could come. I don't have to listen to him. There's nothing stopping me. Except, I don't want to. I want to listen. I want to feel that release without shame. I want to hear him call me a good girl again, even if I feel like I *shouldn't* want that.

But does *should* and *shouldn't* matter right now? We're the only ones here. And he's going to marry me. I realize that I'm afraid of the future, and how he'll choose to use this against me. But that's not something I can carry. He's hard. He's ruthless. But he's not cruel.

Not the way I was to him.

No one will cry for me because I had to beg for a few orgasms.

I've done far more damage. This is nothing in comparison.

A gasp escapes me, bringing me back to the present, another surge of pleasure washing over me, so sharp it almost takes me over. "Please, can I come?"

"No."

I'm looking up at his face, and he's studying me. There's no anger or cruelty in his eyes. If anything, there's compassion. It raises something into my chest, an emotion that I can't name, amplified by the pleasure in my veins.

"Please." My voice is desperate. "I need to. I can't hold it back."

"You will." His words are at once an assurance and a command, though he doesn't slow his fucking, adding a third finger to my pussy. It only makes it worse. I moan, writing on his hand. I can't see him anymore, I'm blinded with the pleasure. "Breathe," he tells me, and I do. I take one breath and then another, going through the storm of pleasure. Sizzling in it.

Daniel's thumb brushes over my clit in small circles in time with his thrusts, and I can't bear it. I'm right there. I'm so close that I don't think I can take it back. "Please please please please please." The words spill out of my mouth. I beg him. "Please, Daniel, I can't—I need—"

"Okay, Princess." The words are soft in my ear. "Come."

My orgasm roars outward from his fingers, consuming me. I think I scream. I'm aware of nothing but this pleasure flying through me, making me fly. I'm shaking, my pussy squeezing down on his fingers and pouring my orgasm onto his hand.

He doesn't stop fucking, triggering a second orgasm, and then a third like fading aftershocks of an earthquake. It might be the best orgasm that I've ever had in my life, and I'm not sure that I'll ever recover.

When I come to, I'm breathing hard, and I'm no longer on the floor. I didn't even notice Daniel picking me up and holding me close, moving us both to the couch. My head is lying on his shoulder. "Did I pass out?"

He chuckles, the vibrations soothing. "I don't think so. It's only been a couple of minutes."

We sit there in silence for a few moments before Daniel turns toward me, taking my mouth in another soft, aching kisses. "Was that so bad?"

I shouldn't want to be near him, and I can't bear the idea of not touching him. So I hide my face in his neck. "Which part?"

"Any of it."

"The orgasm was nice."

He laughs again. "And?"

I pause, not wanting to say anything. But after everything, it seems silly. I was bared to him in every way just moments ago. There's no reason that I shouldn't be able to talk. To be honest. "You're really going to make me talk about it?"

"I am," he says. "But it doesn't have to be right now if you don't want that."

"You're not going to make me beg to talk about it, are you?"

He shakes his head. "No."

"Good."

I don't say anything more. I don't know how to feel and I don't know what to say. Maybe when he asks me again there will be something else in my mind. But right now my mind is...quiet. Which it hasn't been in a long time.

"The lawyer will be here soon," Daniel says quietly.

That brings me out of my reverie. "I don't have anything to wear. Please don't make me wear this."

He kisses me on the forehead, a surprisingly tender gesture. "In my room, bottom drawer. There are some sweatpants and a t-shirt."

"But it's the marriage lawyer," I say.

He grins, lifting me up and setting me on my feet. "We're getting married regardless, and he gets paid no matter if you're wearing sweats or not."

It's a fair point. "Okay." It's better than being in cum-covered lingerie. I walk toward his suite—the direction he points, but just before I turn the corner, I look back at him.

He's looking out the window, and he's so fucking beautiful. He looks like he doesn't have a care in the world, but he does. He didn't leave me on the floor, he picked me up and cradled me. He took care of me. No man that wants to completely destroy me would do that.

It seems like both of us aren't admitting the whole truth. There's more to this marriage than he's letting on, and I don't hate him as much as it feels like I should.

The words he spoke to me echo in my head. *I'm going to own you, Princess. Heart and soul.*

There's a whisper from deep inside that tells me that he's right. And I'm not sure if I want to stop it.

## 7

## DANIEL

I don't remember the last time I've lost control like that. Ever. Monica drives me crazy in a way that I absolutely can't explain. I want to break her as much as I want to cradle her. The way she hid her head with me just now—seeking comfort even when I forced her to the edge—raises a protective instinct in me that I don't want to ignore. And that I can't afford.

I'm not marrying Monica for sentimental reasons, I'm marrying her to make her pay for her crimes. And it's going to take a lot more than her begging to come to make up for it.

My phone buzzes, and it's my publicist, Rose. I knew that it wasn't exactly going to be quiet with me and Monica, but I didn't think that it would be this fast. "Hey, Rose," I say as I answer the call.

"Do you want a heads up on the questions?"

Rose never beats around the bush and she rarely does pleasantries. But in this case I honestly have no idea what she's talking about. "Questions for what?"

She sighs. "First round of publicity for the launches,

Daniel. Smaller papers from around the Southwest. They're the lead up to the big guns. They're going to show up to your suite in five minutes, this has been on your calendar for a month, we've confirmed three times. I'm in no mood for you to play dumb. Do you want the questions?"

I scrub my hand over my face. "It's been a hell of a last twenty-four hours, Rose. Forgive me for not remembering a drive-by publicity session."

"Just please tell me that you're dressed and I'm not going to see pictures of you in the tabs opening your suite door in a robe and nothing else."

I laugh, "I'm decent. Thank you for the heads up. I don't need the questions."

I hang up, because this is fucking perfect. An illustration for my new bride that I mean business, and that she's going to pay.

My phone buzzes again, and it's Jack calling from downstairs. "Boss you've got some reporters here?"

"Send them up, Jack. And when the lawyer shows up, tell him to wait, please. Something unexpected."

"Sure thing."

I hear the elevator ding and a knock at the suite door a few minutes later. I glance around the suite, and everything seems fine. No stray underwear or something that's going get me into actual trouble. I open the door with a smile and face down the three reporters in my face. "Hi."

A bubbly blonde with a recorder beams at me. "Pleasure to meet you, Mr. Argent. Can we come in?"

I gesture with open arms and the best fake smile that I can muster. "Absolutely."

As they enter the space, she introduces herself. "I'm Lucy Sanford from the Las Vegas Star."

"Mike Bangor, San Diego Chronicle," the handsome man behind her says. I shake his hand. "Nice to meet you."

And finally, "Shelley Pollon, Portland Tribune."

"Welcome to my humble abode."

They settle on the couches in the living room, making themselves at home quickly and easily, as most reporters do. "Can I offer you all some refreshments?"

"Water would be lovely," Lucy says.

"Certainly. Monica," I call loudly. "Can I see you for a moment?"

A few seconds later Monica emerges from my suite in one of my t-shirts. It's so big that it's falling off her shoulder, and she has nothing underneath it. It's sexy as fuck, and I probably could push the neck all the off her thin shoulders and watch it drop to the floor. She hasn't found the sweats yet. So the t-shirt ends at her thighs.

She sees me looking, and blushes pink. "The sweats wouldn't fit," she says. "They keep falling down."

Right now, she's not in the line of sight of the reporters, but she will be. "That's fine," I say. "Will you grab three glasses of water from the kitchen for our guests?"

"Guests? I thought it was just the lawyer." I just smile and raise my eyebrows, and she sighs. "Fine."

I walk back into the living room and settle across from the reporters. "Hit me," I say. "I'm an open book, but unfortunately I don't have a lot of time to give you today."

They nod in unison like their heads are on strings. "Completely understand," Mike says. "I'll start. I'd like to ask about the launch of your newest properties and how you expect them to influence the local—" his eyes slip past me and he freezes mid-sentence. The women's eyes follow his, and I turn to find Monica with a tray of water in nothing but my t-shirt staring down the barrel of three reporters.

"Thanks honey," I say. "I'm sure our guests are thirsty." Monica's face is bright red, and I can see the water in the glasses shaking from here. She glances at me, and I nod towards them. It takes her a second, but she steps forward and hands a glass to each reporter.

Even reporters from smaller papers are still reporters, and they're not stupid. Shelley from Portland is the one that speaks first. "Are you...Monica Blast?"

"Yes," Monica says quietly, looking at the floor.

I catch her around the waist and pull her down beside me on the couch, ignoring entirely the fact that the t-shirt is high enough to show off her thighs and probably her ass. "Miss Blast's presence here and anything she says are strictly off the record. You can ask your questions." I curl Monica in beside me and put my hand possessively on her hip, teasing the hem of the shirt. She's stiff as a board beside me.

"Miss Blast," Mike says, trying valiantly to keep his eyes from her legs and failing. "We've met before, when you were a part of the Miss Nevada competition. You did well."

"Thank you."

I look over at her, and Monica is smiling, but the vision strikes me, because she's smiling but her eyes are filled with pain.

Lucy chimes in. "I'm very sorry for everything you've been going through, Miss Blast. I'm sure it's been hard for you."

Monica's eyes fall to the floor again. "Thank you," she says again. Like a reflex. Automatically.

I shouldn't care. I shouldn't notice that she seems to have shut down and be running autopilot. I shouldn't notice that she's shivering under my hands. I shouldn't suddenly be feeling regret for putting her on display. This is what I wanted. To prove to her that I'm serious about taking revenge.

And it's true, there is a tiny bit of me that feels smug about the blush on her cheeks and her state of undress. But her trembling is getting to me. "Sorry Mike," I say. "What was your question?"

He asks something about the economy and local jobs, and I answer. The others ask their questions too. I don't even remember what they say or what I say because I'm so focused on Monica. She's a shell of herself. Even only knowing her again for the last day I know that. And I did that.

Fuck.

This is not how I imagined that this would go. I had it all planned in my head, how I would revel in her blush and her awkwardness. Right now all I want to do is make her come back. I struggle through the questions, and they seem satisfied, even though I can see the desperation in their eyes wanting to ask questions about Monica.

But they don't. All they do is stare. And finally, I can get them out. I get a ping from Jack asking about the lawyer and I can finally send them away. But Monica doesn't move. Not when the lawyer comes, not when he walks us through the process of applying for a marriage license. All she does is sign the papers, completely blank.

And then the lawyer is gone and she's still gone too. Shit. What the fuck did I step into? It seemed like such a simple thing, a little embarrassment to start my revenge. But I didn't really think. How she's been put on display her whole life. I don't even think I knew about her doing pageants. That was later, after I knew her.

I sit down next to her, and reach out to touch her. She pulls away. "Monica." There's a moment when I can see the tears in her eyes, and it feels like a knife straight into my heart.

I shouldn't care about this. I shouldn't. I should be glad for her tears and that she's getting a taste of her own medicine. But it doesn't feel that way. And after seeing her pure and free and open underneath me, I know in my gut that this isn't who I am. I will make her pay me. There's no question of a debt between us. But I'm wrong to make her pay it to me in front of others.

She'll pay it to me and no one else. I'll extract it from her in borrowed pleasure and begging. I will make her mine.

"It's fine," she says. "We're done, right?"

"Yeah," I say. "We're done." I'm not going to make her talk to me right now. Not if she doesn't want that. I hand her a tablet. "Order yourself some clothes. Everything should be fine on there."

"Okay."

She retreats into the guest room faster than I can even turn to follow her and closes the door. Only time will tell how monumentally I just fucked up.

## 8

## MONICA

For a moment, I sit on the bed in the guest room and just breathe. That was...awful. But not the worst it could have been. There are worse things than sitting by a man's side in a t-shirt. He has the right to do worse to me. In fact, I expect more. I agreed to it.

Daniel was right on one count: the lawyer didn't give me or my clothes a second glance. Though clothes would be generous. I'm wearing nothing but Daniel's t-shirt and the reporters got a good look at me.

I guess my passport and other things had been delivered while I was getting dressed, because they were all there when I just signed the papers. It all seemed very simple. As easy as signing nothing.

And now it's done. Normally it would take several weeks to receive a marriage license. But given who Daniel is, I shouldn't be surprised that the lawyer told us it would be ready either tomorrow or the next day. So fast.

Is this something I really want to do? After that? I know, deep down, that if I refused to marry him, Daniel wouldn't make me. But it's not something that I should be doing just because I'm afraid of losing everything. Or because I'm afraid of him exposing me for who I was. He'll do it again. Tears swim in my eyes, and I blink them away. Come on, Monica. It's not that bad. It's worth it, besides, I *will* lose everything.

As soon as I have the thought, I know that it's bullshit. It's more than just that at play. I can't explain the crazy chemistry between Daniel and me. Embarrassing incident in front of reporters aside, I can't get breakfast and what we did out of my head. I want more of that. Of him. And I feel stupid that I don't even care about being exposed. That it's a price I have to pay and if he can make me feel that way again, I'll gladly pay it over and over.

And as we spoke to the lawyer, there's no penalty for either of us to call it quits down the road. I intentionally ignore the little twist in my gut at that thought. That's it then. I am marrying Daniel Argent, and I can't even pretend that I don't want to do it. There's so much history between us, so much baggage. But there's something here that we need to explore together. Both of us.

I'm still in his t-shirt, and it smells like him. Like the desert sun and cedar soap. After the lawyer left, he handed me a tablet and told me to go crazy. Not in those words, but that was the implication. The tablet already has all of his accounts loaded into it for purchasing things, and I need a whole new wardrobe. But honestly, I don't know what kind of clothes I need.

Taking the tablet, I walk through the living room into the office that Daniel is currently occupying. He's typing away on a laptop, looking as calm as ever. It feels strange to enter this space. It reminds me a bit of what my father's office used to look like, and the reversal is strange. But Daniel is not my father. I know that. Daniel would never do some of the things that my father has done. He would never intentionally cause lasting harm. He would never not care that his actions had cost others their lives.

He looks up at me. "Are you all right?"

"Yeah. I just don't know what I need." He gives me a questioning look, and I explain. "What kind of clothes do I need to be your wife? Am I going to need a lot of gowns for openings? Suits? Is there a way you'd like me to look?"

Daniel stares at me for a moment before standing and coming around the desk to me. "Is that how you see me? As someone who wants to tell you what to wear and control your appearance?"

I shake my head. "Honestly, I don't know. I don't know where I stand with you. I don't know why you want me. I keep trying to make sense of it, and I can't. One minute you're making me beg for you, and the next, you're showering me with gifts, and the next showing me off half naked to reporters. It's not exactly the clearest line of logic."

He sighs. "You're right."

I blink. "I'm sorry? You're admitting that I am right about something?"

"I'm not perfect," he laughs. "And I'm more than willing to admit that what this is, is complicated between us. So let me be clear now." He takes the tablet out of my hand and sets it on the desk before pulling me close. It's strange how comforting that motion feels after such a short time. "I already told you this part of it. When we were younger, I wanted you. Even though I hated the way you treated me, and what your family did to mine, I never stopped wanting you. You are the star of all my fantasies, and I hated myself for it. I didn't understand why I couldn't just let you go. You were never going to want me. Never going to be good for me. But it didn't matter."

A peculiar feeling gathers in my chest. I had known that Daniel had a crush on me, but it didn't matter that much to me. When I was young and naïve, a lot of boys had crushes on me. It was normal to me. But to hear that his was deeper, that he had such a desire that went beyond what he should have felt given my cruelty, makes me ache with sadness. I wish that I had known. Perhaps if I had, and we had been together before now, maybe both of our lives would have been different. Maybe they would have been better, and maybe they would have been worse, but we'll never know.

"When I saw you at that poker table," he says, "all of that came rushing back to me. I thought I had let that part go, that I had taken all that desire and anger and turned it into something else. It's how I made this life. But it hadn't let me go.

"Do I want you, Monica? Yes, I do. I don't think I ever stopped. Is there a debt to settle between us? Yes, there is. But you owe that to me and to no one else. I was wrong to do that to you just now—never should have exposed you in that way. You're *mine* and I didn't realize how much I wanted that. It's not my intention to marry you and make you the laughingstock of the world. You are going to be my wife, and I take that seriously. I'm sorry that I embarrassed you. I hope you can forgive me, and I know that I'm not going to humiliate you publicly again." Tears come to my eyes again, and I have to close them. Daniel pushes his hand into my hair and tilts my face to his. "I need you to hear me when I say that. I want you, you're mine, and I'm sorry."

He kisses me then, and it's soft and fierce at once. It makes me tingle and ache with emotion that I'm afraid to put a name to. I'm dizzy with it, and I have to cling to him just to remain upright. I can't breathe, and it's not just from the kiss. Fuck, what is happening to me?

I absolutely believe his apology. I feel it in my bones, that he means it. His fervent lips on mine leave no doubt. He won't do that to me again, and the relief makes me able to breathe. I was willing to suffer it, but I would much rather just suffer for him, as fucked up as that makes me feel.

He's breathing hard when he pulls away. "And I'm not going to stop making you beg me," he says. "Not yet, at least. For all the things between us that need to be settled. And you know that there are a lot of them. You owe me a debt, and you're going to pay it privately. To me and only me. I like it when your face flushes with embarrassment when I tell you what to do. I like to see you out of control. I like having power over you." He pauses, looking down at me seriously. "But I think you like it, too."

"I don't," I whisper. But we both know that it's a lie.

"Not the kind of power where I'd hurt you, or where I control what kind of clothes you get to wear. You know what I'm talking about."

I can't look at him anymore. I press my forehead to his chest to hide my face. "I shouldn't."

"Why not?"

"Because."

"Because women have to be strong?" He simply holds me, letting me hide. "You've been plenty strong, Princess. I know there are things that you haven't told me, and I know it's been worse for you than you're letting on. It's okay to be angry about it. And it's okay to enjoy not having to make any decisions for a while. It's also good to be able to ask for what you want even if you feel like you shouldn't want it."

Anxiety grips my chest, and I wrap my arms around his waist. "Can I ask you something?"

"Anything."

"What happens when you've had enough? When you

decide that the debt is paid and you want to move on? Because you're making it very hard to hate you, and if you're going to take what you want from me and then decide that it's over, I need to hate you. I need that or I won't survive it."

There are so many things that he could say, and I thought that I was prepared for all of them. But not this one. His words are soft, but firm. "It will never be paid, Princess."

To most people, those words may sound like a death sentence. But I hear them for what they really are: a declaration. Whether or not we ever view ourselves as equal in the things we've done to each other, he's not letting me go. Something small eases in my chest, and I relax into him. He has no exit strategy, no plans to drain me and drop me and leave me for dead. And that, for right now, is enough. I sense that he wants to say more, but neither of us are ready for that. We both know it though. Both feel it.

"To answer your first question," he says, "I don't give a shit what you wear. You could parade around the streets as naked as Lady Godiva and that would be fine with me, even though I might be a little jealous. Will there be events? Yes, probably. You can wear whatever you want to them. Buy the most expensive dresses you can find if that's what's going to make you happy. But don't think for a second that I am going to make you dress a certain way."

Oh. "Okay."

"Why do I get the feeling that this is a first for you?"

Because it is. When I was a kid, I always had to look a certain part, play the role of the heiress for the Blast Dynasty. You can't escape being the daughter of one of the world's biggest developers. And when I was in beauty pageants, it was the same. A certain way to look, a certain way to be, a certain way to act. Even when I was with Martin, he always requested certain looks. Demanded more than requested most of the time, and it didn't matter. He left me anyway. Though I try not to think about him. "It's just... unexpected," I say. "That's all."

"You're not telling me everything are you?"

I shake my head. "No, I'm not."

Daniel kisses my forehead. "That's fine. I hope you'll tell me some time. But buy what you like. I wanted to take you ring shopping tomorrow, and there will probably be cameras—there usually are when I'm out in public. It's just something to be aware of, but I want you to wear whatever makes you happy."

*What makes me happy?* I wonder as he lets me go and sits back at his desk. I definitely have a lot of things to look through in order to decide. When I get to the door he calls my name. "Monica?"

I turn around to face him.

"I really do mean it. What makes you happy, not what you think will make me happy."

I nod before leaving the office. I didn't realize such a simple question would give me so much to think about. I hadn't realized how many restrictions had been placed on me in that way. What do I like to wear? I don't think there's ever been a time in my life when I've been free to choose without anyone else's opinion involved. And in the last two years, that hasn't been a matter of opinion, but a matter of survival. Beggars can't be choosers when you're shopping at thrift stores. So what do I want?

I have no fucking idea. But I am very excited to figure it out.

* * *

Later that afternoon, I'm surrounded by racks of clothing in the suite's living room. I had chosen a few things that I thought I liked, and I showed Daniel. Instead of congratulating me, he immediately picked up the phone and asked one of the boutiques to send over a selection and some assistance for me. I told him that he didn't have to do that, but he shook his head. "I think you need it. Plus, Alex is a fantastic designer. She instinctually gets style, and if you don't find anything you like in her current collection, she will happily design it for you. Hell, she might just design it for you because she wants to. She's been begging me to get married for years so that she can dress someone close to me."

That makes me laugh. "Why?"

Daniel smirks. "Because she says that no one who looks this good in a suit should be single."

"She designs all of your suits?"

"Every single one. I've never met another person who was able to take the feeling that I wanted from my clothes and interpret it so well. Once I discovered her, I never looked back."

So now the living room has been transformed into a makeshift salon. It's still a little mortifying to be in Daniel's sweats and T-shirt, but Alex just shakes her head and waves a hand when I mention it. "Don't even worry about it, honey. When I'm through with you, you'll have the best damn wardrobe anybody has ever had in their life. I've been hounding Daniel for years for this."

"He said as much."

Alex is shorter, with cropped red hair and chunky jewelry. She's wearing a flowing, flowery dress which might look juvenile on somebody else, but on her it looks like she's part hippie, part healer, part goddess. She has a sketchbook tucked under her arm and a pencil behind her ear, and she's already looking at me like she knows me. When she notices me watching, she smiles. "Sorry," she says. "Hazard of the job. I'm always thinking about how clothes are going to look on somebody. How do you see your style?"

One of the girls she brought with her hands me a flute of champagne and I take a sip, it helps soothe the nerves. "I honestly couldn't tell you. Most of my life my style has been dictated for me, and I don't know where to start."

"That's okay," she says. "We can start with the basics. We'll go through the clothes we have here, and you tell me yes or no about whether you like it, if it's a mix you tell me what you like. I'll get a good idea for what you're drawn to."

And so as we go through the clothes, I don't think about anybody but me. And I try not to think too hard about it. I stay away from anything that reminds me of my pageant days, and if something looks interesting to me, I point it out. Halfway through the second rack of clothes, I'm beginning to see a pattern. Simple cuts, solid colors, and stylish lines. I like some patterns, and some details, but I'm not drawn to them the way I am the other things. Perhaps it's because of all those things that I was forced to wear that were rich and over-the-top. I was always forced to be girly, and to present the right image. No one seemed to notice that they didn't tell me what the right image was.

Alex doesn't do anything but smile and nod as I point out things. There are even a few things on the racks themselves that I like so much that I immediately pull them out to try on. "This feels very much like a Pretty Woman moment," I say.

She chuckles. "Yeah, I suppose so."

The things I've chosen are comfortable and simple, without being drab. There's some lovely trousers, sweaters, and tailored shirts. Thrown into the mix are a few flowing numbers as well. I seem to be drawn to cooler colors, with rich blues, creams, and greens making up the majority of my choices.

The last rack of clothes are more formal. There are some beautiful gowns, and I wonder if I should choose any of them. I don't have to, I know. I took what Daniel said to heart and I know that he'll be happy no matter what I choose. But even if I didn't love the pageant lifestyle, I still really like dressing up. I like the power it affords me as a beautiful woman, and I like the way I can command attention. Also, it can just be fun.

There's quite a few on the rack that I like, but then I come across one that takes my breath away. It's a pale blue silk, and at first it almost looks like a nightgown. But it's not. The thin straps flow over the shoulders and down, catching the material in such a way that it drapes in one long line. The seams are artistic, lying on diagonals and almost giving an Art Deco feel. There are just a few silver details along the hem and the neckline to add some sparkle. But something about it calls to me, and Alex sees it.

"You need to try that on right this second."

"How can you tell?" I ask her.

"Because I've seen that look before. That is the look of love at first sight with a dress. Once somebody has that moment, there's pretty much no going back. So try it on."

I take the dress into the bedroom and slip it on over my shoulders. Yeah, Alex was right. I love this dress. It makes me feel ethereal and beautiful, like something out of a fairytale. And when I come out of the bedroom, the look on everyone's faces confirms it.

"Yeah, that's the one. Working to get that altered for you right away."

They already took my measurements when they first arrived, and I can feel a couple of places where the dress isn't perfect, but it's pretty close. Alex looks down at her sketchpad. "I think I've got a pretty good idea of what you're looking for. Over the next couple of days, I'm going to put together some sketches for you and you can look at them. In the meantime, do you feel like you've got enough pieces to choose from for the next few days?"

I nod. But I'm unable to look away from the image of myself in the mirror. It doesn't seem like me. And yet it does. It seems more like me than anything I've ever worn before. Suddenly, I feel eyes on me. In the mirror I see that Daniel has walked in behind me. His eyes are glued to me, and I meet his gaze in the reflection.

The room seems to go still around us, and even Alex and the assistants go quiet. I turn around to face him, unable to stop the blush from creeping up my cheeks. I'm not sure why I feel embarrassed in this moment. Perhaps embarrassed isn't the right word. But I feel... vulnerable. It's like I've taken off some sort of mask and he is seeing through it for the first time.

But that's not true either, because he's already proven that he saw through it all along. I have taken off the mask, and it's my first time being seen. I don't know how to feel.

Daniel slowly crosses the room to me. I'm standing on a little pedestal in front of the mirrors, and it brings me just a little closer to his height. He stares at me when he stops in front of me, and I feel the urge to fidget nervously. Only my pageant training keeping me from doing so. "What do you think?" My voice sounds more worried than I want it to, but I want him to like it. I want him so desperately to see what I see when I put on this dress.

He doesn't answer me. Not with words. He just reaches

out, slipping a hand behind my neck and kissing me softly. But it doesn't stay soft. It grows into an inferno. The kind of kiss that should never be done in front of others, but I don't even care. And this time it's not just him kissing me, I am kissing him back. Until we are engulfed in each other, his arms wrapped around me so tightly that I don't want him to let go.

"Does that mean that you like it?" I ask.

"I love it," he says. "You look like you."

He'll never know how perfect an answer that is.

"If you're going to keep doing that," Alex says, "at least let her get out of the dress so that we can take it to alter it."

Daniel smiles. "Just one second, Alex." He leans in, and I let him kiss me again, the assistants in the background giggling as Alex sighs.

## 9

## DANIEL

The marriage certificate in my hand is beautiful. It's flashy in a way that only Las Vegas can achieve. But I don't care, because it's here. Barely twenty-four hours after we put through the paperwork and here it is. All we have to do is sign both of our names and we will be officially married. The question is, will Monica be willing to sign the paper before the actual wedding? I don't want to wait, and I'll give her whatever wedding she wants. But I want her to be my wife. And I want that moment to be sooner rather than later.

I can recognize that I'm falling down a spiral that I will never be able to come back from. I can't pretend that I fully understand the need I feel to make her fall in love with me. I said it so that I can justify all the years that I wanted her, when I was young. But is that really it? Is it to make me feel powerful? All I really know is that what I said yesterday to her in my office was true. I want her. More than I've ever wanted anything.

More than I want revenge. More than I want to expand my business. More than my own preservation. When I walked out into the living room and saw her wearing that dress, my stomach dropped through my shoes. Not because she was suddenly more beautiful— she is always beautiful — but because she was shining. She seemed vibrant in a way that I've never seen her, and I was just a moth to her brilliant flame.

We had dinner last night in the dining room. We had pleasant conversation, and for the first time it felt easy between us. A glimpse into what our life could actually be like. It was a struggle for me not to think about our experience at breakfast, but I managed.

And when it was time to say good night, I was proud. Monica asked for what she wanted. She asked me to come into her room with her and take her. And when I told her no, even though she seemed disappointed, she didn't fight me. She let me kiss her, and I swear the way she went pliant against my body made pulling away from her the hardest thing I've ever done in my life. But I told her that I wouldn't fuck her until she was my wife, and I intend on keeping that promise. But I swear, if we aren't married soon, I might not be able to.

I slip the marriage certificate back into the envelope it came in, and put in the inside pocket of my jacket. I'm taking Monica out to look for rings today. I want her to have an engagement ring even though it's not technically an engagement.

I hear the door to her room open, and I meet her in the living room. She's dressed in a simple blouse and trousers, so different from what I'm used to seeing her in. In high school she was always wearing sundresses or revealing crop tops and low-riding jeans. It didn't occur to me until she asked how I wanted her to look that maybe she hadn't chosen her image. It still makes me angry to think about, the idea that her parents would have used their teenage daughter for their own gain. But given what I've read about her father in the past day or so, it doesn't seem like anything is beyond him.

The clothes she chose for herself suit her so much better. She would look stunning in literally anything, but there's power in being able to choose your appearance. There's a reason I enjoy wearing suits tailored for me. I like the satisfaction of knowing that I look powerful. I imagine that Monica has the same desire.

Her hair flows simply around her shoulders, and I want to see it spread out on my pillow. I want to have her drag it over my skin so I can feel its softness. She smiles shyly. This is new for her. Hell, it's new for me. Navigating the situation is delicate, but I think we're doing okay so far. The feeling in my gut when I see her can't be ignored, but I refuse to let it rise to the surface. Because it's too huge, too vast, and it terrifies me.

"Good morning," I say.

"Morning."

I'm the one that closes the distance between us and pulls her in for a kiss. I can't get enough of her lips. I always wanted to kiss her. That was the first fantasy my mind always jumped to— kissing her. I never want to stop. She tastes sweet like fruit. "You look lovely," I say as I pull away. Her cheeks turn the light pink that I crave to see when I give her a compliment. Monica is so pale that she blushes easily, and I won't pretend that I don't like using it to my advantage. "Thank you," she says.

I hold my arm out to her, and she slips hers through. "Shall we?"

I like the way it feels to have her on my arm. We're going to Cartier today, and people already know. They know because whenever I go shopping anywhere in Vegas—

which is rare—I have my assistant call ahead and have them clear the place out.

"Did you sleep well?"

She laughs a little. "No. Not really."

"Why not?"

Her cheeks tinge pink again. "Dreams. About you."

"That's an answer that I like to hear."

She glares at me, but it doesn't have much anger to it. "I did ask, you know."

"You did."

She shrugs. "It's not my fault that I had to take care of it myself. Three times."

That comment goes straight to my cock, and I shift myself in my pants as we step into the elevator. My mind is swirling with images of Monica twisted in her sheets, moaning my name in the dark. Fucking hell. I need to marry this woman, and fast. If I didn't have the launch so soon, we would have one hell of a honeymoon. As it is, I will take her on a tour of Vegas hotels to rival anything she's ever seen. I'll fuck her in a different bed every night until every hotel in the city has heard her cry out my name.

And she screams so well—the way that she let go in the dining room yesterday was proof enough of that.

"You're right," I say, voice low. "That was not your fault."

As we step out of my private elevator, Devon and Jack flank us. They are my most trusted security guards, but Monica's words yesterday remind me that I should add more people into my rotation. I've gotten very comfortable, and I never should. I need to rely on other people and keep the net wide.

But today, on my first outing with Monica, I won't take the chance with anyone else.

The casino is full and busy. It's a Friday and people are

arriving from out of town for the weekend. I watch Monica out of the corner of my eye, and she's looking around at the casino, but I can't get a read on what she's thinking. I don't like that. I'm so used to being able to predict people's actions, and a good part of the time Monica is like that too. Until she retreats into herself like this. I'm not sure what causes it, but I don't want to push her too hard. I already know that I'm pushing her boundaries.

"Devon," I say.

"Yes, Mr. Argent?"

"Are there cameras?" I glance at him.

He nods. "Yes, sir."

Monica looks up at me. "Cameras?"

"Paparazzi."

"Oh."

"The car is already waiting," Devon says.

We walk out the front doors of the casino into a wave of sunlight, heat, and flashbulbs. The limousine is already in place, my driver holding the door open for us. I let Monica slide in first and in seconds we're safely ensconced in the car, though I can still hear the reporters asking questions. We just made our public debut as a couple. Monica is a recognizable face thanks to her father—and the reason she's been in such trouble. I imagine my publicist will start fielding questions about it in under an hour. As soon as they figure out who she is. But I'm not going to call her. No comment is always a better policy in the beginning. She won't answer any questions until she talks to me.

"Haven't seen that in a while," Monica says. "Not since..."

She trails off, and I realize that the last time she faced press like that would have been her father's trial. "Are you all right?"

"Yeah," she says. "I'll be fine. You're going to have a lot of people mad at you."

"I don't care."

"I'm serious. People are going to call you crazy. There are going to be people you don't know coming up to you and telling you that you shouldn't be anywhere near me because I'm going to steal your money. Marrying me is likely going to be the worst press that you've ever gotten."

I shrug. "Like they say, there is no such thing as bad press. And my marrying somebody isn't going to change the fact that customers like my casinos. And once we get the wedding taken care of, and all those pictures hit the media, I'm sure that there will be no problem."

Monica nods, but I don't think she actually agrees. She's biting her lip, and her hands are fidgeting in her lap. I reach across the seat and grab her hand, and she startles a little. "Do you trust me?" I ask her.

"I do," she says. "It's just that I think that you barely know about what happened with my family, you don't understand how bad it really is."

It's a fair point, and I don't discredit her worry. All I can do is help distract her from it. "Well, don't think about that now. That's not the point of what we're doing today."

She smiles. "I know."

"Would you like an engagement ring? I'd like you to have one, but if you don't feel like we had enough of engagement, I would understand."

Monica thinks about it for a second, and I appreciate the fact that she's actually taking time to think about it and not just saying yes to me. "How about we get there and we see what the selection is?"

"Fair enough. And the same rules apply today as yesterday. Only choose what you actually like, not what you think I would like."

"I can do that," she says.

Using the hand that I have trapped, I pull her closer to me. The amount of satisfaction that runs through my body when she comes without resistance and leans her head on my shoulder is overwhelming. I feel like I could take on the world, conquer anything. The media, every business deal in the book, fuck, I think I could climb Mount Everest in this moment.

Traffic on a Friday in Las Vegas is always a cluster fuck, so it takes us a while to get to Cartier. But when we pull up, Monica goes still. "Cartier? We're going to Cartier?"

I press a kiss to the top of her head. "Where else?"

"You know that I honestly hadn't thought about it? I just assumed... I don't know. Maybe I thought you had some exclusive secret diamond dealer in the basement of one of the hotels."

I laugh. "I won't pretend that I don't have diamond connections, but meeting in hotel basements is generally unpleasant."

I get out of the car first and there are photographers here as well, but not as many as there were at the hotel. Not everyone has the connections to find out that I closed down the store. I help Monica out of the car, and then I hold her close as we walk toward the doors. Devon and Jack are already flanking us, so the photographers don't get closer than they need to to yell their questions. But they already know who she is. That was fast.

The voices blend too much together for me to catch entire questions, but I get the gist. What are we doing together? Why are we here? How do I feel about her father's crimes? And of course, the question that she just warned me about, and that I knew would come up, why would a billion-aire like me associate with someone so closely tied to scam-ming and cheating?

A Cartier employee holds open the door for us, and we slip inside. The walls are well insulated here, and as soon as the door shuts the noise cuts off like we pressed pause on the radio. Monica looks uncomfortable, and I know that she heard what the reporters were asking. I turn her toward me and use a finger to tilt her chin up, but she still avoids my eyes. "Look at me, Princess." She does. "When I said I don't care about that, I meant it. I know it's not an easy thing, but try not to let it get to you. They don't know you."

"You barely know me," she says. "They've been following me for years."

"Has any of what they've said about you ever been true?"

She laughs. "Barely."

"Then fuck them all," I say. "They're doing their job and they're trying to get a story. But there's no story for them to find. Now let me buy you some jewelry."

That does the trick. Monica smiles a little, even though it doesn't reach her eyes. I think I can get her to forget, at least for a little while. The atmosphere at Cartier is quiet and peaceful, and we have total freedom to look at or try on anything that we want. But for the first little while, as we're roaming around, Monica doesn't try on anything. She comments on how beautiful the diamonds are, and how she kind of likes one thing or another but nothing truly grabs her attention.

I give her a little space, looking over the jewelry myself. There are some pieces here that cost more money than some people make in a lifetime. But Monica is worth that. And I've always had a rule— though she doesn't know it— whenever I buy an item of luxury, I donate the same amount to charity. I don't think I could live with myself any other way. I spent too much of my life poor to blindly spend money like it's water. I'll have to find out if there are charities she would like to support before I make the donation for this.

I stop when I see a necklace. It's that similar feeling to when I saw Monica in the casino for the first time. A gut deep knowing of 'that's the one.' The necklace itself is silver, a beautiful twisting chain. And on it, a teardrop diamond contained in a swirling silver cage that looks like a blooming flower or vines. It's incredibly understated compared to some of the other jewelry in the store, but that's the one. I think that she'll like it.

I raise my hand for one of the attendants and she comes rushing over. "Put this on our bill," I say. "And have it sent over to my suite at the Brazen Hotel. Today please."

"Of course, Mr. Argent." She immediately starts working on packing up the necklace, and I move to rejoin Monica before she notices that I bought something. I find her near a display of rings in a corner of the store. And when I see what she's looking at, I know I made the right decision. All these rings are silver, and understated. The display itself is in the corner, like it's been hidden away because this style is less popular.

"Do you like these?" I asked.

Monica nods. "I think they're beautiful."

"What do you like about them?" I want to know why she's drawn to things.

She tilts her head, still looking at the rings, and thinks. "I like that they're unassuming. Not that there's anything wrong with being the center of attention, I'm just tired of it. Everyone's already going to know that we're married. I don't need to remind them with a ring the size of my head," she says. Then she smiles and adds an afterthought. "Plus, they're pretty."

"They are that," I say. "Which one?"

She points. "I want to try that one." Her finger is over the glass, hovering over a simple silver ring with a round diamond. The band twists and curls around the stone on either side. The attendant who's been shadowing her steps up and opens the display case and pulls it out. He holds it out to Monica on its display rod. She goes to pick it up but I stop her. "Let me," I say.

She does. I take the ring and hold her hand, softly slipping the ring onto her finger. A thrill runs up my spine, like déjà vu but looking forward. Like feeling what I'm going to feel in the future. The ring fits almost perfectly. It's a tiny bit loose.

"What you think?"

She's staring down at our joined hands, and I can feel her shaking a little bit. I don't blame her in the slightest, this feels like a lot even to me. The ring looks perfect on her hand. I hope she agrees.

"I love it," she says.

I love it too, but the emotions welling up in my chest leave me no room to say it. I point to the simple silver bands — one bright and one dark— that rest next to where Monica's ring was. "Can we see those?" I ask.

The attendant brings out the rings, clearly a matching set, and I put the bright one on next to the ring Monica is already wearing. I slip my own on, though it's a bit too tight.

Monica is staring at her hand, completely enraptured.

"I think choosing these is going to be a lot easier than I thought it would be."

"Yeah," she breathes. "I can't imagine anything else."

I look at the attendant. "We'll take these then. Can they be sized today?"

"Yes, sir. We'll take your measurements. It looks like they're pretty close. For you, Mr. Argent, we'll have them done in an hour."

"Perfect," I say. "We'll go get lunch and come back."

He quickly takes our measurements and we test a couple of ring sizes making sure that everything is comfortable. And when we're satisfied, he disappears into the back without another word.

"Is that it?" Monica asks.

"That's it. What do you feel like for lunch?"

She shakes her head. "Honestly I have no idea. It's been a while since I got to choose food based on desire and not economy."

I pull her close as we make our way back to the door. "Let me rephrase the question then. What's your favorite type of food?"

"Italian," she answers without any hesitation.

"How do you feel about pizza?"

"Pizza sounds fucking brilliant," she says.

There are fewer reporters outside than when we entered the store. It makes sense. They don't need a conclusion to print a story about me and Monica shopping at Cartier. Even a tabloid reporter on their first day could make a connection and a story out of that and a picture of us entering the store. There are still some that stuck around though, asking to see the new jewelry. Granted, we didn't exit with anything. Let them make of that what they will.

I take Monica to an amazing pizza place in Vegas. It migrated over from Chicago, and serves some of the best deep dish pizza around. As a bonus, the owners of the Las

Vegas establishment know me, and we won't have a problem getting a table that's more private.

They pride themselves on anybody being able to come to their restaurant and not be harassed, which is something that I greatly appreciate. Especially with the amount of local press that I get. National press not so much, thankfully.

Monica doesn't say much, and I don't push her, even though I wonder what's going on inside her head. We order a pizza, and it comes quickly. We've been seated in the back of the restaurant, and aside from the person who brought our order, not even the waiters are allowed back here.

Our silence is a testament to how good the pizza is. "Would you like a drink?" I ask.

"Yes," she says, "that would be great. Thank you."

"What would you like?"

"Iced tea?"

I stand, and button my suit coat.

"The waiters aren't allowed back here while we're seated," I say. "So I'll go ask for it."

She holds out her hand as if to stop me. "You don't have to do that."

"I want to," I say, leaning over the table and pressing a kiss to her forehead. "It's no trouble."

There are TVs on in the main restaurant, and as I walk around the corner the name 'Blast' catches my ears. Surely Monica and I aren't being reported on live television yet, so I looked toward the TV with trepidation. Sure enough, the newscaster is commenting on the latest round of charges against Monica's father. Apparently his lawyers have exploited some flaw in testimony and evidence to get him an appeal on some of the charges.

That old familiar anger wells up in me, but then it passes through me and doesn't take hold. It used to be that whenever I heard anything regarding the Blasts I would see red.

So much so that I eventually began to tune it out, and started avoiding all mentions of the family and the media. Which is why when Monica showed up, I had no idea what had happened. I don't regret not knowing. I had held such a grudge that watching that drama unfold would have filled me with the kind of glee that I can't explain, and thinking about that embarrasses me. I certainly wouldn't be capable of having the relationship with Monica that I'm trying to have now if I had known about all the charges.

But the anger passes through and out, and it's a completely relieving feeling. Without even trying, I seem to have let go of some of that anger. Even when I talk about that debt with Monica, I don't mean it literally. At least not anymore. I may have started this for revenge—and I'm going to have my fun, and my way, with her—but it's not my main motivation anymore. Just in the short time we've had this deal, she's shown me that she's not who I thought she was. And I'm captivated by the person she's shown me: quiet and introspective and beautiful.

I hope she knows that. I hope she understands that when I told her I wanted her, it's the truth.

It stuns me that so much could have changed in such a short time, but I'm not going to fight it. Change is good, and it's clearly something that I want if everything can turn so fast.

I look again at the television and frown. What would Monica's life have been like if that man were not her father? I guess we'll never know, but we all have our own struggles. I'm getting the picture that Monica's life was not as easy as I always believed it to be.

Grabbing the tea, I go back to the table. "Just so you

know, your father was just on the news. Apparently he's getting an appeal in some of those charges."

Monica's face goes pale, she looks down at the table. "I hope he doesn't get it," she mutters. And she suddenly looks at me, eyes desperate. "You know I had nothing to do with it right? I had nothing to do with any of it. I didn't know that he destroyed the neighborhood until later. I didn't know he was stealing all that money."

I nod. "I know."

"Okay."

"Do you want to go get the rings?"

"Sure," she says, looking relieved to change the subject. "I just need to use the restroom first. I'll meet you outside?"

I nod. Outside should be just fine. Reporters knew better than to bother this place, or they'll have the cops called on them. Closer to the car I'm sure we'll have more of a problem.

It doesn't take long, and when Monica steps out of the restaurant, I drink in the sight of her basking in the afternoon sun. When I reach out for her hand, she gives it gladly with a smile, and we start to walk toward the car. We swing by Cartier and pick up the rings without incident, but I don't let her see the rings. Not yet. I have a plan for that. "We're not taking the limo back," I tell her. "I wanted to drive, so I had them drop off one of my cars. Security will still follow us in another car, but I wanted us to be alone."

Monica raises an eyebrow. "We were alone in the limo."

I lean down and whisper in her ear. "Not so alone that if I choose to make you scream, we wouldn't be heard."

"How are you going to do that if you're driving?" she asks, but she's blushing.

"I'll figure out a way."

Suddenly, Monica goes utterly still, stopping in her

tracks. At first I think she's tripped, but she standing solidly. Her expression is sick and pale, and if I'm guessing correctly, full of fear. I follow her gaze and I encounter somebody that I haven't seen in more than a decade. I don't remember his name, but it's Monica's old boyfriend. The one who slammed me into a wall of tools in the shop.

Why is Monica afraid? Is she afraid that he will see us together? Or for some other reason?

Just as quickly as she froze, she's trying to move, pulling on my hand. "Let's go, I don't want to see him."

I don't hesitate. I start pulling her faster in the direction of the car, but I don't move fast enough.

"Monica?"

She's shivering, but stops. Looking at her face, he would never know that anything was wrong. She pastes a brilliant smile on, the one I recognize as her mask and speaks. "Martin? Wow, it's been such a long time."

"Not since you went and hid under whatever rock you been living under," he says, the smile on his face cruel. "Finally decided to show your face?" I'm stunned. I don't know what I was expecting, but it wasn't that. Suddenly, Martin looks at me. "I know you, don't I? You're the guy that owns all those casinos."

"I am," I say. "I'm also the guy you put into a wall senior year of high school."

His cruel smile suddenly turns into a sneer. "Couldn't land her in high school so you're trying again when you're rich and famous? Congratulations, Monica, on finding yourself a new sugar daddy."

I look to my side at Monica, and she's looking at the ground. Never in my life have I seen her look this small. She's no wallflower, and she certainly hasn't had any problem telling me to fuck off when she thinks it's necessary. Suspicion and anger work their way up to my chest. What did this man do to her?

Martin keeps speaking. "Let me give you some free advice. Stay away from this poisonous bitch and her family. You give them everything in the world, and they won't even be fucking grateful."

Monica turns toward me, not looking, just instinctually seeking what she feels is protection. Something roars inside me. Satisfaction that she views me as safe, and fury that she feels unsafe at all. And somehow, this prick is still talking.

"I should have ruined you when I had the chance," he says. "But it looks like you've done a pretty good job of that yourself, haven't you? How's the law career going? Anybody want to touch you? I didn't think so. Nobody will ever want a whore like you."

I snap, releasing Monica and springing forward. Before I can even fully comprehend what I'm doing, I've punched Martin in the mouth. Then he's on the ground and I punch him two more times. I grab him by the shirt and haul him up so that he can see Monica. "Apologize."

"Never," he says. "I'll never apologize to that bitch. Go figure she's got you wrapped around her slutty little fingers."

I hit him again, and stand over him. "Apologize, now."

The sight of him on the ground, laughing as blood pours from his nose is disturbing. "No," he says. "You can keep hitting me, but it's never going to happen. Just remember that I was the one she fucked when you weren't good enough. All you'll ever have is my sloppy seconds."

I reach for Monica and she takes my hand without hesitation. There are cameras and bystanders. It's Las Vegas, of course there are. Pictures of this will likely be on the Internet within the hour. But I don't regret a thing.

I pull out my cell phone on the way to the car, and call

my publicist. She answers on the first ring. "Daniel, I've been getting—"

"There is a massive shitstorm coming your way," I say, "and we're going to talk about it and decide what to do. But I will be unavailable for at least three hours. Call me when that time is up." I don't give her a chance to respond before I hang up. Devon and Jack get us to the car, and split off to their own. They'll keep watching to make sure we're not being followed by any curious onlookers.

I open the passenger door for Monica and she slides in, and I go around to the driver's side. I probably frightened her, and I need to explain myself. I apologize. I also would like to know what the fuck happened, if she's willing to tell me. "Listen," I say. "I'm sorry."

But before I can get anything else out, Monica is clamoring into my lap. She settles over me, straddling me the same way she had in the dining room. And she's kissing me. This isn't the kiss to get around what I've told her, or to punish me, or anything else. This kiss is pure fire, and we're both going to be consumed by it.

She pulls away, staring at me with what feels like awe. "Nobody has ever done that for me," she says.

"What are you saying?"

She kisses me again until we're both breathless. "Nobody has ever stood up for me like that. In my whole life, let alone since everything happened with Dad. Thank you."

Sick dread and anger on her behalf fill me. "Never?"

"Never. And especially not Martin. He wanted me to be somebody that I wasn't. My parents pushed us together because his family is rich. They wanted us to get married, and they wanted it so much that it was easier just to stay with him than to get insults like that thrown at me. I tried to leave a few times, but he made me believe that nobody else would ever want me. I finally did leave him when I went to law school, and took hell from my family for it. Martin was furious. He said he felt like he had wasted the best years of his life on someone who was nothing but a whore, who wanted a sugar daddy to pay for everything. And when everything came out into the open with Dad, he was the one who spun it to make it look like I'd been a part of it all along."

My hands tighten on her waist, and I have to know. "Did he ever hit you?"

"No," she breathes. "But I think he eventually would have. He came close."

I slide my hand behind her neck and pull her in to kiss her. "I thought I had scared you."

"And I thought you might believe him."

"Why?"

She hides her face in my neck. "Because everybody else did."

I hug her close to me, and every plan I had for the rings and the marriage certificate goes out the window. I have to do this now. Sliding my hand between our bodies, I retrieve the envelope inside my suit. "I was going to wait until later for this," I say. "But I can't."

"Is that—"

"Yes," I say. "I swear to you, Monica, you can have whatever kind of wedding you want. But I don't want to wait. Marry me. We have the rings. We have the papers." I look into her eyes when I ask. "Marry me. Be with me." The last words are like a whispered prayer.

She doesn't say anything for what feels like an eternity, but then she nods. "Okay." And she kisses me again, this time soft and slow. She climbs back into her own seat, and I fish the rings out of my other pocket. Taking her hand, I slip the engagement ring on her finger followed by the wedding ring. Just like in the store, I feel a telling sense of something bigger. The rings fit perfectly this time.

Her small hand slips the ring on my finger, and neither of us speaks as we sign the marriage license. Monica takes a shuddering breath. "It's official."

"It is." I haul her toward me back over the center console to take her mouth. Now that she's mine—really mine— I don't want to wait. "And we need to get back to the hotel."

She laughs against my lips. "Why?"

"Because I want to fuck my wife," I say, voice rough. "And I want the first time I do it to be in a bed."

Monica shivers, but there's a small smile on her face. "Drive fast," she says.

## 10

# MONICA

I never knew that I could hate traffic this fucking much. All I want is to be back in the hotel with Daniel letting him peel me out of my clothes so he can finally do what I've been dreaming about. I sneak a peek down at my finger again.

*Married.* I just got married. That's insane, and yet it's not.

I knew the second that Daniel punched Martin in the face that that was it. I wasn't exaggerating to him that no one has ever stood up for me. Everything was always my fault. With him. With my parents. With the people I was trying to get jobs with. It didn't matter what it was. It was my fault. End of story.

I remember time and time again when a teacher blamed me for something, my parents never listened to my side of the story. If there was a bad story in the news about me, that was my fault. If something went wrong for Martin, it was somehow my fault. I never really understood why no one thought to check or ask if it wasn't.

Until Daniel.

I felt sick, seeing Martin. I thought that this was over, that Daniel would listen to him and suddenly it felt like all the hope in the world had disappeared. Until he threw that punch. I don't think he'll ever know how much it meant to me, as fucked up as it is to love someone for punching someone else. I freeze internally, and look down at my ring again.

Is it possible that I love my husband?

It might be. I don't want to admit that because it feels too fast and too big and the circumstances of getting here too awful and strange.

But I might.

Finally, we pull into the garage and Daniel practically springs out of the car. He tosses the keys to Jack, and pulls me close against his body as we walk. We're moving fast, but not fast enough to avoid the swarm of reporters just inside the casino. Daniel isn't deterred in the slightest. He pulls me through them with Devon on our heels, and I don't even bother to hide my face. They got plenty of pictures earlier, and everyone is already going to know.

It doesn't bother me as much anymore, because I know that Daniel isn't going to blame me for whatever they say. It will be awful things, for sure. But we can worry about it later.

Devon stands in front of the elevator doors as they close on us, blocking the photographers from joining us. They disappear into silence, and neither of us can wait anymore. Daniel has me up against the elevator wall in a second, kissing me like he might die if he doesn't. *I* might die if he doesn't. I moan into his mouth, and my tongue dances with his. I spent all last night breathless and panting, dreaming of him. I want everything that he can possibly give me.

"You remember the rules?" he asks.

"You're really going to make me beg you to fuck me, Daniel? We just got married."

He pulls my shirt to the side and bites my shoulder, gently, but hard enough to send tingles downward. I'm already wet, and I want him to bite me again. Bite me everywhere.

"I want to hear my wife beg me to fill her pussy with my cock. I want to hear her begging to suck it. To taste me. So desperate to come that she'll do anything for it."

"Fuck," I barely can speak before he's devouring me again, and when the door opens into our suite, we collapse inside. Clothes are flying, and I can't get to his room or my panties off fast enough. Suddenly we're at the door and I'm naked and he's naked and holy *God* he's beautiful. This is the first time I've seen him without clothes, and I was right about one thing—he's not the Daniel I remember from high school. Every inch of him is hard and sculpted, and for one breathless moment, we stare at each other, before he has me in his arms, carrying me to the bed. He's so *big*, and I love that he's everywhere, pinning me down with his weight, stroking and kissing and teasing me until I'm thoroughly surrounded underneath him.

Daniel places one hand on my chest, and moves to straddle my torso. My hands fall on his thighs, marveling at how even this part of him is toned and muscular. And his cock...that's right in front of me. So close. Rigid and extending toward my mouth like a beacon. I want him to take me again, fucking my throat and then my pussy. The way he's looking at me—utterly filled with lust and possessive fire—makes me squirm, pressing my thighs together to relieve the ache between them.

"Ask," he says, his voice so raw it sends need racing through me. My nipples are harder than I've ever felt in my life, and I wonder what it would be like to feel his cock in between my breasts. At some point I'm going to ask, but right now I want to taste my husband's cock.

*My husband.*

"Please," I say, arching underneath him. "Please let me suck your cock."

Daniel guides the tip of it into my mouth, thrusting hard. He fills me instantly, stretching my lips and slipping to the back of my throat. I groan, looking up at him. His perfect body towers over me, and his eyes devour me. "Christ, Princess," he says. "Your mouth feels good."

He thrusts into me, and I close my eyes, relaxing into the feeling of delicious helplessness and the taste of his cock in my mouth. Rich and deep and wholly him. I suck hard, using my tongue as best I can, and he groans. "Later," he says, "I'm going to fill that sweet mouth with cum and watch you swallow it, wife. But my first orgasm married to you is going to be deep inside your pussy."

I used to think it was impossible to be so turned on from words alone. I was very wrong. Daniel pulls his cock out of my mouth and lowers himself, poised to thrust into me. "I'm clean," he says. "Haven't been with anybody in months, and I've been tested."

"It's been years for me," I say, "and I don't want anything between us. Not now."

He fits the head of his cock against my entrance, and hesitates, then he looks at me. I realize what he's waiting for. He's not going to fuck me unless I beg him too. "Daniel, please, fuck me," I say. I have no qualms about it. I want this. Want it so badly that I could scream. And it doesn't feel bad with him. Asking for what I want, knowing that even if the answer is no, it won't be met with derision or disgust.

Daniel doesn't need to hear me ask it twice. He thrusts in, slowly sinking into my pussy until he can't anymore. We both groan with satisfaction, and my pussy stretches deliciously, accommodating the exquisite invasion. He's so big that he fills every part of me with electrifying heat and friction. "God, Daniel," I moan.

He leans over me so that our faces are close. "I know," he says. "I know." And then he kisses me, sealing us together in a way that feels permanent and overwhelming.

Gripping my legs, he raises them around his waist so that he can plunge deeper still, and I can't breathe. Pleasure swirls from my pussy outward, making me gasp and shake. I'm so turned on that I'm already close. Waiting to go over the edge and fall into that bliss. I can't fucking wait.

Daniel thrusts his hips, setting up a rhythm that takes my breath away. Every stroke brushes against my clit and I'm spiraling higher and higher, and I can't even breathe because he's still kissing me. "I can't hold it," he says. "Come with me."

He thrusts harder, pounding into me and sending explosions of pleasure through my core. He groans, and his cock jerks inside me. He comes, spilling himself and pure liquid heat into me. It's enough to make me lose it, and I cry out against his lips as I come, shuddering underneath him.

The orgasm is deep, pulling pleasure from places inside me I was unaware of, seeping through me and drowning me with it. I'm lost in the pleasure sea, carried by the tide. I don't want to come back up.

Our breath mingles as we come back to each other, still tangled, still connected. My hands are grasping Daniel's shoulders and I can see my wedding rings. We're married. This is forever.

And for the first time, I know that I want it to be. I don't care about how we got here, or the fact that I felt like I didn't have a choice. I did. And I made the right one. My head is spinning because I love Daniel Argent, and it feels like it was always meant to be.

Daniel's eyes tell me the same thing, and we don't need to speak. We just kiss, eyes open, wrapped around each other. Finally, Daniel whispers. "Hello, wife."

"Hi, husband." The word makes me laugh, happiness bubbling up in my chest like a giggle. But then he consumes my mouth again, and there's no more laughing.

Already all the way inside me, Daniel hardens again. Feeling him stiffen, filling me up and stretching me as he grows is so intimate, so delicious that it makes me wet all over again. This time we move together, hips thrusting to meet each other. Slowly at first, barely a movement. Gently experimenting with what feels good. Daniel moves his hips to hit different angles inside of me until he finds one that makes me gasp. It lights me up like a fucking candle, and suddenly pleasure spikes sharply through me.

He slips his hand under my spine, grasping my ass and tilting it higher, slipping in a fraction more. Until I can feel his balls pressed up against my ass and there is no more of him to take. I'm stuffed full of him, so much that my breath is short. He stops and holds himself there, letting me ease into it. Letting me accept it.

It's more than just his cock that I'm accepting—it's him. His full place in my life and in my body. I'm taking all of him with no exception, and he's showing me that.

He kisses my neck, biting it gently and soothing the bite with his tongue. Again and again until I'm moaning, squirming on his cock, wanting more and begging wordlessly with my body. But he doesn't move. He's telling me no. To wait until he says yes, and I try.

But I want more. I want to scream and fuck and be taken. But I make myself still, looking up at him as he looks down at me. He smiles, soft and full of warmth. "Good girl, Princess."

And then he fucks me.

Before he hadn't. He was holding back, because this is *more*. He pulls all the way out and slams all the way back into my pussy. Long, brutal strokes that hit me deep and make me cry out in ecstasy. They make me blind with it, and there's nothing I can do but take it.

Daniel grabs my wrists and pins me to the bed, adding to that feeling, and I love it. I love not having to think and just being allowed to feel, free from the fear that someone is going to take this away from me.

Pleasure rises up in a wave, and I gasp, ready to let go, but Daniel shakes his head. "Don't come."

"Please?"

"No, Princess. You're going to take it. You're going to wait until I say you can, because I'm asking you to."

I bite my lip and hold on, fighting back the overwhelming wave of pleasure that's pulling me under. It's slicing into me like a knife, every thrust making it sharper and me more desperate to reach that mindless bliss on the other side. The longer I hold on, the deeper that well of pleasure becomes, until I am begging him. Nearly screaming. I won't be able to hold it off anymore, and he knows.

"Now," he whispers in my ear, and I explode. Pleasure bright as a nova blasts through me, sizzling through every nerve and crevice. My pussy locks down on his cock, and I can feel him coming with me, heat inside me spurring my own climax on. It's so good that I feel like I might die.

It takes long minutes for me to recover, hauling in breath after breath of air, mind completely blank. It's Daniel's soft press of lips to mine that brings me back all the way. He's still on top of me, still inside me, and I love the comforting weight of him. Like one of those weighted blankets they sell for people with anxiety.

Daniel laughs. "What?"

"What?"

"You just called me a weighted blanket. What does that mean?"

I hadn't realized that I had spoken out loud. "You know those really heavy blankets that people sleep under and it makes them feel nice? This is like that."

"I'll take that as a compliment," he says.

"Good."

His weight lifts, and I make a sound in protest which he smothers with a kiss. "I'll be right back."

I can still barely keep my eyes open, so I rest, hearing the soft sound of water, and then the feeling of the mattress dip and his heat near my skin. A soft cloth gently cleans me, and I'm so tired that I can't even find it in me to be embarrassed that he's doing it. But my eyes won't open.

He stretches out beside me and pulls me to him, covering us both with an actual blanket. His arms wrapped around me are warm, and it's pulling me down quickly into sleep. "I'm sorry," I say.

Daniel's voice sounds amused. "For what?"

"For being so tired."

He chuckles, and I can hear it under my ear. "I'm not," he says. "I fucked my wife well. I'd almost be insulted if you weren't tired."

"Okay," I say, snuggling closer to his chest. This is nice. Martin never wanted to hold me, nobody ever did. But not anymore. Now, this is what I want. To lie in the arms of my husband, and simply sleep.

I feel Daniel's lips kiss my temple before I drift off. I think he says something...but I can't be sure.

**11**

---

## DANIEL

I wait until Monica is entirely asleep before I even try to move. Even after I know that she's asleep, I don't really want to go. I want to keep holding her, and feel her soft body against mine. But I also know that if I don't deal with the repercussions of the media, it will be bad for both of us. It hasn't been three hours yet, but my publicist, Rose, is probably having a shit fit.

Very gently, I lift my arm out from underneath her, and replace it with the pillow. I make sure that she is cradled with pillows and blankets before I leave the bed. Monica's breath is deep and even, and I am extremely satisfied that I can make her pass out so thoroughly. I hope that I can fuck her to sleep like that every night of our lives.

After she had already drifted off to sleep, I told her that I loved her. I know that I'm a coward for not saying it to her face, but I wanted to hear how it sounded out loud first. I like saying it. I like the way it feels.

Pulling on some sweatpants, I noticed my wedding ring. I don't normally wear rings, and this is going to take some getting used to. But I'll gladly do it.

I retrieve my suit jacket from the floor in the living room, and get my cell phone out of the pocket. I also get our signed marriage license out of it so that I can give it to my lawyer. As predicted, my phone has half a dozen calls and just as many texts from Rose. I pour myself a drink before I dial her number, and sit on the couch. I could easily go for a nap just like Monica, but this needs to be dealt with. The media never sleeps.

Rose speaks as soon as the line connects. "What in the ever-loving fuck did you do, Daniel?"

"I thought I paid you enough money not to swear at me."

"I will swear at you as much as I damn well please when you do something like this to me."

I cringe. "How bad is it?"

"Let me summarize it for you, shall I? He was spotted this morning going into a diamond store with the daughter of one of America's most infamous white-collar criminals. Not even an hour later you were seen getting into a fight with this woman's ex-boyfriend, son of one of America's most powerful industry tycoons. And when you reached the hotel, the pictures show you with the same woman, but now you're both wearing wedding rings. How bad would you say that is?"

"The fight is bad," I say. "I don't see a problem with the rest of it. So I got married? Who cares."

"A lot of people fucking care, Daniel. You are one of the country's youngest, best looking entrepreneurs. Oh, and you happen to be a billionaire. You don't think people are going to freak out a little bit about you marrying the daughter of someone who swindled thousands of people out of their livelihoods and savings?"

"She had nothing to do with it. I don't see how that matters."

Rose sighs, and I can practically see her rubbing the bridge of her nose. "If you had perhaps called me first? We could've gotten out of this. We could have implemented the plan that would've turned public opinion. Had something like a big wedding, repackaged her into America's sweetheart. The wronged bride finally has her happy ending."

I take a sip of my drink and look out over the city. "We're going to have a wedding. It's going to be beautiful, and I'm sure the pictures will recover some of that damage. But we are not going to repackage her as anything. Monica is who she is, and she spent her entire life being packaged to suit other people's palettes. I'm not going to do that to her."

Rose doesn't speak for a moment, and when she does her voice is soft. "Is this for real, Daniel? Like, is this the real thing? If it is, you know that I'll do whatever I can to help you. But if this is some drunken mistake that's going to end up in a divorce that will rival Charles and Diana, tell me now."

"It's the real thing," I say. "Monica and I knew each other when we were younger. We reconnected and we decided to get married. It's as simple as that." I leave out the rest of it, because winning someone's hand in marriage in hand of poker isn't good PR. Plus, it's nobody's business how or why we reconnected.

She sighs. "Fuck. Okay, the video of you sucker punching that guy is already all over the Internet. People were filming."

"Of course they were," I say, taking another sip of my drink. "It's Las Vegas. They probably thought it was some kind of show until later."

"It doesn't matter what they thought," she says. "All that matters is that that video will be all over the news tonight, if we don't have something to combat it with. What the hell did he say to you to make you hit him?"

I tell her. Every single word. It'll be burned in my brain for a long time. But I think I can actually hear Rose smiling. "Well, shit. I can definitely work with that. That's an easy spin into defending her honor, and it will lay some of the groundwork for the rest of it. And you guys are already married?"

"Yeah," I say, nodding even though she can't see me. "We signed the papers today."

"I wish you would have waited. It's way easier to spin a love story when you have something to look forward to."

I laughed. "Spin all you like. Frame it like this: we met up again after not seeing each other in a decade. We fell head over heels in love, and we didn't want to wait to get married for the sake of the wedding. But we'll be planning one so that we can celebrate with all our family and friends."

"And by 'all our family and friends,' I hope you don't mean her father."

I finish off the last of my drink. "I doubt it," I say, "but I'll have to check with her."

"Please, Daniel. I'm serious. There are some things that spin won't fix, and this is one of them. I can separate her from him in the media. I can make it a different thing. But if he's at the wedding that's a psychic link between her and her father that I will *never* be able to break. Got it?"

"Yeah," I say. "I'll talk to her."

"And you're going to have to tell me the real story," she says.

I shake my head. "That is the official story."

Rose sighs again. "You know better than this. I can't protect you fully if I don't know the whole story. And the

NDA we've got will literally bury my soul under a ton of rubble if I break it. So stop pussy-footing around and tell me the story."

I do, though I'm not happy about it. I do lessen a few of the details of the rift between Monica and me, but for the most part, I'm honest. Especially about the part where neither of us expected it to go this well or this fast. Thankfully, she's all business.

"Okay. Good. I think I can work with this, but while I've got you on the phone, I want to review some media requests —some for this and some not—and see if you want to do them."

"Sure."

Just then I hear the door behind me open, and I turn on the couch to see Monica coming out of the bedroom. She's not wearing a stitch of clothing, and fuck, if looking at her isn't the best thing in the world. It hasn't been that long, but she must have woken up and found me missing. She still looks sleepy and peaceful, and I smile at her as Rose starts listing off the first media pitch.

I think that Monica is going to come and sit with me on the couch, but I'm wrong. Instead, she comes and stands in front of me, and without any prompting, sinks to her knees. My cock goes instantly hard. Impossibly hard, given that I've already come twice today.

When I wanted to humiliate her, I wanted her like this. I wanted her to feel what it was like to be beneath someone else so thoroughly. Now I don't *need* that, but seeing her kneel in front of me is hot as fuck.

And she doesn't waste time either, pulling at the waistband of my pants until I lift my ass and let her pull them off me. She strokes my cock up and down, making it jump and jerk because it's already so hard and ready. When she takes me into her mouth, I have to clench my jaw so I don't moan into the phone. But I can barely think, barely breathe.

God, she's so good at this, and when she sinks down so my cock slips into her throat, I almost come right then. "Rose," I say. "Can I actually call you back?" I don't wait to hear her answer before I hang up. "Fuck, Princess."

She grins, batting her eyelashes at me. "Am I being a good wife?"

"The best wife," I tell her. "I think I can reward you."

"Oh?" Her eyes are sparkling. "How?"

I lift her off her knees and pull her onto the couch. "Trust me." She squeals but doesn't protest. "What are you doing?"

Leaning over her, I part her legs, and lick her pussy from top to bottom. God, I could live off that taste. The sweetest desert there is. "Only one catch," I tell her, pulling away.

"What's that?" Her eyes are already glassy with pleasure.

I fit my cock to her lips and push into her mouth, and she takes me eagerly. "Don't stop sucking my cock. Not even when I make you come."

She sucks me hard, and I have to close my eyes for a moment. I'm going to have just as much trouble concentrating as she is. I know that. I lean back over her pussy and lap at the wetness there. I love how quickly she becomes aroused for me. The idea of fucking her mouth didn't turn her off in the slightest. I am a lucky man.

I seal my mouth over Monica's clit and suck it as hard as I can. She groans on my cock, and I like the way it feels on me. "Keep moaning for me, Princess," I say as I lick my way to her entrance. She does, making sounds that I've only ever heard in porn, and these are so much better because her mouth is gagged with *my* cock.

Her moans only grow louder as I invade her pussy with my mouth, plunging deep and tasting her sweetness. I work her in long, lazy strokes. Enough to arouse her but not enough to send her over. Not yet.

Circling her clit with my tongue, I move faster, sending her higher and higher. Until she's screaming around my cock and not even sucking anymore because she can't. I know she can't. I consume her like she's my last meal, and I swear to God that I hope she is. She's shaking under my mouth, suddenly coming, flooding my tongue with her flavor. I drink all of it.

And I keep going, licking and sucking and eating her until she goes over again. My cock falls from her lips and she can't stop moaning and saying yes. I love the sound of her climax, the way her voice goes raw and rough and uneven. I can't get enough of that sound.

I release her, pressing my cock back between her lips. "Keep sucking," I say, pressing deeper, and she does, but I'm in control now. I press myself completely into her, slipping into her throat until her lips seal around my base. "How do you like your reward, wife? Is this a good one, for being an excellent wife?"

A moan is all she can do to respond, but I watch as her pussy grows wet before my eyes. Yes. She likes this. I close my eyes, thrusting into her mouth and throat, and I let my orgasm rise up from the deep. The texture of her tongue against my skin is driving me mad, and the sensation of popping in and out of her throat is sending me over the edge.

"Fuck, Monica, I'm going to come down your throat." I hold her head still, and she opens wide, letting me pump in hard and fast. I'm fucking her mouth exactly the way I would her pussy, and it's the hottest thing I've ever seen.

Monica reaches up, and touches her clit, her beautiful fingers circling and teasing. On her hand, is her wedding ring. Fuck. She sucks down on my cock, and I plunge deep one more time, orgasm ripping through me from the base of my spine. Monica sucks hard, swallowing everything I give and more, cleaning my cock and drawing out the pleasure for every last second.

Flashes of light burst behind my eye. Nothing but light as I poured myself into her naughty mouth. And she deserves an even better reward for that. I snatch her wrist away from her pussy, sealing my mouth over her clit and licking it. Again and again and again until she's gasping and shaking and saying my name. Her hands are gripping the couch so hard that her knuckles are white, and I smile against her skin.

One more for good measure. I press two fingers into her pussy, finding that rough patch inside that makes her scream, and lick her again. It only takes seconds before she's coming, voice echoing off the walls of our suite.

And then she melts, body going limp, and I catch her, lay her out on the couch and spread out beside her. Her eyes are sleepy again. "Hi," I say.

"Hi," she says. "I woke up and wanted more. Now I'm sleepy again."

"Well, you can have more anytime you want."

She blushes pink and smiles. "Do you have to call that person back?"

I stroke my hand down her side, savoring the feeling of her skin. "No, it can wait. We covered everything important."

"Okay."

"Should I take you back to bed?"

She grins shyly. "For a nap or more sex?"

"I don't see why there can't be both," I say, standing and lifting her into my arms.

She giggles, and it's the best damn sound in the world.

## 12

## MONICA

I wake up, drowsy and feeling nearly drugged. I'm not, it's just because I didn't get very much sleep in the night. The morning sun is shining through the windows of the suite, and I stretch under the sheets feeling the sweet ache of my body. I'm wearing nothing but my wedding rings, which is the same way I've woken up for the last three days. I don't think there's been more than a few hours between our stints in bed. He can't keep his hands off me, but I'm exactly the same.

We've basically been in hiding. On the advice of his publicist, public outings together haven't been on the top of the priority list, which is totally fine for me. I'd far rather stay in our hotel room and fuck my husband than deal with reporters. She thinks it'll be good to give the public time to accept us as a couple while she works spin. It's given me some time to think about the wedding, since that's important for public image. Daniel insisted that I do what I want with the wedding, and don't let anybody push me into something I don't want. Which is nice.

But I haven't been looking at any of the media or the

news, because I don't think that would make me feel good about anything. And the fact that Daniel has been intentionally avoiding that subject confirms it. It's fine. I'm used to it. I'm sure they're calling me a gold digger and all kinds of other names. But if Daniel doesn't care, neither do I. Or at least I try not to.

I roll over, and unlike the last few days when I've woken up, the bed is empty. That's too bad. I'm sure that if Daniel were here, just rolling over would have him pulling me against him and we'd end up entangled for the next hour or so. Instead, I reach for my phone on the nightstand. There are a lot of messages. There have been over the past few days, especially from people that I haven't heard from in years. Suddenly, being married to a billionaire makes me interesting enough to talk to again.

I don't answer those calls. If you weren't willing to be my friend when I was going through the hardest period of my life, then you don't get to be my friend when things are suddenly looking better. There is a message from Alex's assistant, confirming that she'll be over at noon to deliver my wardrobe sketches and talk about them with me. And to possibly start talking about the design of my wedding dress.

There's a message from Daniel too, and I click it open.

*Sorry I'm not there to help you wake up this morning. Duty calls. As much as I wish I could ignore everything and stay in bed with you, people are starting to get mad that I'm ignoring their messages. Call me when you have the chance.*

I dial his number and roll over so that I'm on my stomach and hugging a pillow. I can pretend that I'm lying on

Daniel's chest. It won't work though, because Daniel is a furnace, and I never get enough of his warmth. The phone rings, and after a couple, he picks up. "Hello?"

His voice is so fucking sexy over the phone, deeper than it normally is. I miss it already. I know it's partially the honeymoon phase, but it's also just him. "Hi," I say, my voice still scratchy with sleep.

He chuckles when he hears it. "Good morning, Princess."

"You told me to call you."

"I did," he says. "Besides wanting to hear your voice since I couldn't be there to wake you up, I wanted to ask you something."

"Shoot."

"How would you feel about having dinner with my parents tonight?"

My stomach jolts. He's mentioned a couple times of the last few days that he wants me to meet his parents again. Under normal circumstances, meeting somebody's parents wouldn't make me as nervous as this does. "Are you really sure they want to meet me?" I ask. "I can't imagine that I'm in their good graces. Especially right now."

"They actually don't know yet," he says. "They try not to pay attention too much to gossip columns. More than one misunderstanding about me and my life has come from that, so they generally get their news straight from me. So if they have seen a story about you, they won't believe it until I tell them."

"And you don't think they're going to be pissed? If you were that mad at me, I can't even think about how much they feel."

His voice is gentle. "They will love you because I love you. I swear."

"Okay," I say, even if I'm not sure that I believe it. "What's the dress code for this dinner?"

"Monica," he says, and I can practically hear him rolling his eyes. "How many times I have to tell you that you can wear whatever you want?"

"I know that I can wear whatever I want. But this is your parents and I want to make a good impression. Please just give me some kind of direction. Are we going to their house? Are we going to a fancy restaurant?"

"Their house. It won't be fully formal, but not fully casual either. Wear something nice that you feel comfortable in, that's all I ask."

"Alex will be here in an hour," I say. "She'll help me pick out something, I'm sure."

"Yes, she will. I have to go," he says. "And I likely won't be able to make it to pick you up because there's a lot of things to catch up on. I'll have a car pick you up to take you to my parents' house at 6 o'clock, okay?"

I nod, even though he can't see me. "Yes."

"I wish I was there with you, Princess."

"Me too."

The silence hangs in the air, full of our unspoken words. Finally, Daniel says, "Think of me today." And he hangs up.

As if I'm going to do anything but think about him. Especially when I get up and get myself into the shower. I'm filled with memories of the last shower together, which was yesterday. Daniel ended up on his knees in front of me, making me come over and over again before he took me against the wall. Fuck, I want that again.

I don't know when this rabid desire will stop, and I'm not sure that I want it to.

The table full of breakfast food is there again, and I eat my fill before getting dressed. I never see anybody put the food out, but I hope I do at some point because it's delicious.

Alex shows up right on time, breezing in with a bag full of fabric samples and a big sketchpad. "Hello, hello," she says. "I see in the past couple days a lot has happened between you and Daniel."

I can't stop the blush that rushes to my cheeks. It's true, though. "Yeah," I say. "I guess so. I've been kind of ignoring the news."

She looks at me sympathetically. "I would say that's probably a good call."

I laugh. "Yeah."

She sits down on the couch and deftly changes the subject. "So, ready to see your clothes?"

"Absolutely."

Just like Daniel had predicted, Alex has created a collection of clothes that suit me more perfectly than I could have chosen for myself. She took all the elements that I liked of the clothes that she showed me and expanded on those. Every sketch is tasteful, delicate, and understated. "Well," I tell her. "Daniel said that you were good, but this is more than I ever imagined."

"Thank you."

"All of these are perfect."

She grabs her bag of fabric samples and lays them out on the coffee table. "Just tell me which of these fabrics you like the best, and we'll use a combination of them."

We spend a few minutes going through the different fabrics, and she explains to me things about them like how they feel, how they're made, and the benefits of some compared to others. When we finish, I'm feeling much more relaxed. "Alex, I was wondering if you would help me put together something for tonight. I'm going to have dinner at

Daniel's parents' house, and I want to make a good first impression."

She raises an eyebrow at me. "You don't think you'll make one?"

"I don't know." My hands fidget in my lap even though I try to keep them still. "There's a lot of history between our families, and not all of it is good. I know that Daniel doesn't care what I wear, but I'll feel better if I'm wearing something that I feel confident in."

She places her hand on my shoulder. "In that case, I'm happy to help."

I hear my phone ringing in the other room. Only a few people actually call me now, so it might be important. "Excuse me," I say. "I'm going to answer that, and then I'll be back and we can talk about it. Maybe we can also talk about my wedding dress."

Alex beams. "Girl, I have so many ideas for that."

"I can't wait to hear them," I say, as I exit the room.

I left my phone in the bedroom while I took a shower and forgot about it. I'm half expecting to see Daniel's name on the screen, but the number that I see makes my blood run cold. It's the number for the correction center where my father is being held. I almost don't answer it. I almost convince myself that it's okay to let him go. But decades of me trying to win my father's approval win out. I press answer. "Hello?" I hear that familiar recorded message that I'm receiving a phone call from an inmate. "Accept."

"Hello, Monica."

I swallow. "Hi, Dad."

"It's been a while since I heard from you. Thought I'd check in on my favorite daughter."

I hate that that makes me feel good, I hate that even

though I know that he's not calling to actually catch up on me, that I wish he were. "How are you doing?" I ask.

"I can't complain for being in jail," he says, laughing. "There are worse things."

Every time I talk to my father, I'm reminded of how he could pull off all the things that he's done. He has an undeniable charisma and charm. Only he could make being incarcerated sound like a fucking vacation. "I'm glad you're doing well."

"But tell me about you," he says. "Are you kicking ass, my baby girl storming the law offices of the world?"

I laugh. "No, Dad. No one will hire me. Because of you."

He makes a sound of disapproval. "That's too bad. I can make some calls for you if you like," he says. "Even from in here I still have influence. Besides, I may not be in here for that long. If you haven't heard, I have an appeal."

"I heard," I say quietly.

"Excellent," he says. "Then when I get out of here, you can come work for me."

I know that telling him no isn't going to do anything. It didn't do anything when I was younger. He doesn't acknowledge the word if it's not the answer he is already looking for. "Thanks."

"So," he says, "we have lots of newspapers in here. I've seen some very interesting pictures of you."

"I try not to pay attention too much to what the newspapers say about me. What have you seen?" I can see him in my head. Stretching out lazily, pretending that he doesn't care about what he's saying, when he's really circling in for the kill.

"Pictures of you with a wedding ring on. I never thought that my sweet baby girl would get married without talking to me first. But then again, I suppose I haven't been the best father for the past few years. I know who that man is," he says. "Daniel Argent. Didn't you go to high school with him?"

"Yeah, I did."

"Rumor is he's very successful now," he says. "Though he's generally a pretty private guy. But I have my connections, I know about Brazen Casinos, and all of that wealth."

I put a smile on my face so that my voice will sound cheerful. "I did what you always wanted. Married a rich man who can take care of me."

"And I'm very happy for you. I hope that you're having a good time with him. But remember, your loyalty should always be to your family."

I shiver, even though the room is warm. "What you want, Dad? I know you're leading up to it. Please just tell me."

He lays it on thick. "Is that any way to talk to your father?"

"Get to the point," I say, frustration rippling through me. I don't know what he wants, but I know it's not good for me.

"Fine," he says, his voice no longer the friendly salesman. "You know what happened to the money. It's all gone in those stupid fucking lawsuits for those stupid fucking people. I need some to help fund my appeal, make it flow to the correct people, and set me up once I get out of this place."

I knew it was coming, and yet the shock still hits me with unbridled force. "Are you seriously asking me for money?"

"Why do you sound so surprised? I made your life good for you. I gave you everything in the fucking world. I took care of you for years longer than any father should have to take care of a child, and you lived in luxury. All I'm asking is for little bit of money from your new husband who's wealthier than we ever were or could be."

"How can you ask me to do this? You've stolen millions of dollars from people. You're responsible for hundreds of deaths. You haven't even spoken to me in years until it was suddenly convenient for you. How do you think that this is okay?"

I can see his expression in my head, and it is an ugly one. "Do you know where your mother is?"

My heart stutters in my chest. "Do you know where she is?"

"Of course I do. She's my wife. You don't think I know where she is? I'll tell you, if you help me."

No matter what my parents have done, they are my parents. I love them even if I shouldn't. I miss my mother. I haven't seen her since the day my father was arrested. I looked for her, but I didn't have the skills or resources to find her. Plus, with all the media attention on me and my father, I didn't want to put them onto her scent, in case something bad might happen to her. "Plus," he says, "you owe me. You know you do. I got you out of trouble more than once, and you wouldn't be where you are without me."

I think back to that day in high school. As it so happens, it was the last day that I ever spoke to Daniel. The one that he referenced right before he punched Martin, in the car shop where Martin shoved him into a wall. He was drunk, we were pulled over. I wasn't drinking, but the cops didn't care. I would've had a DUI on my record if my father hadn't intervened for me. I never would have been able to become a lawyer. I can't find my voice to speak.

"He doesn't even have to know," my father whispers. "He has so much money, that a couple hundred thousand dollars won't even make a dent. I'm sure the Bar Association would be interested in that little development, as well as some others."

My throat feels like it's going to close up and I can't breathe. I still can't talk. But somehow I can't say no. All the things he says are true. I don't know what other things he's referring to, but nothing at this point would surprise me. My father forgets nothing, and he always makes sure that people are somehow indebted to him.

"I'll make sure you get the information of the bank account where I want the money. I am not ineffectual simply because I can't walk down the street. If I don't get this money, you'll not only be disbarred, you'll never work again. I will poison the water so thoroughly that you'll never be able to show your face again."

The line goes dead, and I feel like I just walked into a blizzard. My entire body is covered in shivers, and I'm shaking. I don't know what to do. I want to know where my mother is, but more than that, I don't want to lose everything that I worked for. No matter that the water was already poisoned, I was hoping that I would still be able to work while married to Daniel. I don't doubt that my father has the kind of influence that he claims. There are plenty of bad men in the world, and I'm sure that he still has many of them as friends.

Could I actually do this? Steal from my husband, who I'm actually starting to love? Is my father right? Would Daniel even know?

I can't believe that I'm actually considering it. But I already lost everything once, and I don't want to lose everything again. After everything that I did to him, has Daniel actually let it go? Is there any possible way that he could really love me after all the bullying? After my father and my family destroyed his life?

There are so many instances I can think of where I was cruel to him and I didn't have to be. I *wanted* to be. Because I thought he was insignificant. Because my friends and my family all told me that being poor was some kind of crime. The day that I broke his Game Boy flashes in my head, and it makes my heart hurt. I'll never be able to erase the pain and betrayal that was on his face that day. I knew it was wrong as soon as I did it, but I was so angry that he had dared to look at me. That he had dared to want me. I never apologized for that, and I don't know that I'll ever be able to.

Daniel hasn't said that he loves me, even if he is showing it with his actions. A deep fear takes root inside me that perhaps it's all just a game. Perhaps he's like my father in that way, playing everyone for his own advantage. Maybe he's showering me with affection and gifts and sex so that he can do even worse to me.

I know it's wrong. Deep down in my gut, I know that it's wrong, but I can't shake it. In my hand, my phone buzzes. It's a text message with a bank account and routing number. It doesn't surprise me that he's able to get a cell phone to text me in prison. It surprises me even less that he's able to speak about blackmail on a monitored prison line and know that nothing will happen. If anything, it proves that what he was saying is true.

Alex is still waiting for me, so I place a smile on my face and walk back out into living room. "Okay," I say. "Sorry about that."

Looking up from her sketchbook, Alex looks at me. "Are you all right?"

I nod. "Of course."

She looks at me as if she knows I'm lying, but I plaster on my best smile and sit down next to her again. "Let's talk about the wedding dress."

13

___

## DANIEL

I arrive at my parent's home before Monica does. That's intentional. She wasn't wrong this morning when she expressed nervousness about how my parents might feel about her. I certainly was the one with the heaviest grudge against the Blasts, but that doesn't mean that my parents were unaffected, or that they'll necessarily be happy to see me with Monica. I'm hoping that if I break the news to them personally, and explain my change of heart, that they'll be on board.

Plus, it's been a while since I've seen them, and I'm banking on them being happy about that to soften the blow. My mother seemed surprised when I called her to ask for dinner, but happily agreed. She said she wanted to talk to me, which means they likely have seen the gossip and want to know what on earth is going on with me. I didn't lie to Monica. There was a moment a couple of years ago when the tabloids reported that I had gotten married, but it wasn't even close to true. So my parents always wait for confirmation from me for big life news.

However, I have to admit that the pictures of us with wedding rings on are particularly damning.

The house I bought for my parents is in the same upscale suburb as my own, though I don't spend much time there. I generally prefer to be at my hotel, closer to the casino in case something needs my attention.

I could've afforded something much bigger and grander for them, but they're happy here. And that's the most important thing to me. After all they did for me when I was a kid, trying their hardest even though we were broke more than half the time, I just want them to be happy.

When I pull up, my mother is already opening the door, but I take a second to text Monica and tell her that when she gets here, she can just come inside. The smile on her face is huge. "You really need to come see us more often, honey. You're getting too used to staying in a hotel."

I pull her into an embrace. "I like my hotel, Mom. I can get food delivered whenever I like."

She snorts. "It's not as if we live on the moon out here. You could have whatever you want delivered."

It's a fair point. My dad appears behind her, and I hug him as well. "How are you, son?" he asks.

"I'm really good. I swear. In fact, I'm probably the best I've ever been."

My father's eyebrows raise to his hairline. "Really? Because I could've sworn I saw a video online of you punching some guy in the face."

I laugh as we walk into the house together. "If you'd heard what the guy said, you'd have punched him too."

"Tell me," he says, "and I'll let you know."

"I'll get to that," I say, handing my father a bottle of wine that I've brought with me. "I have something else that I want to talk to you guys about first."

My parents share a look which confirms all my fears. They've heard about the marriage, and right about now they're wondering if it's true. But my mother smiles and takes the wine from my father. "Well, take a seat," she says. "I'll pour this, and we'll talk about it."

I let myself relax in one of the large comfy chairs in my parents' living room while my father helps her with the glasses. It's a nice red wine that I've brought. Generally, I'm not a wine guy, and neither is my dad, but we'll drink it for the sake of my mother. Wine helped her rediscover the joy in life after she recovered from her illness and things were looking up. She's become quite the connoisseur, and I have to keep her on her toes with what I bring her when I visit.

"This is quite good," she says as she enters the room. "Not the best thing you've ever brought me, but close." She winks as she hands me the glass.

"Well, you have to keep me on my toes," I say. "I can't be slacking off on my wine game."

My parents both sit across from me, and suddenly I feel like I'm in some kind of interview. "So." My father levels a look at me. "What do you have to tell us?"

I take a sip of my wine and clear my throat. "I need to invite you both to my wedding. I don't have a date yet, but you'll be the first to know when we do. It will be soon."

My mother looks at me like I've grown a second head. "So it's true?"

"What are you referring to?" I need her to be specific. There are so many things that the media has been saying, that I don't want to just say a blanket 'yes' when she could be talking about anything.

"I saw the pictures of her with the ring on but I didn't want to assume."

"It's more than that, actually. We are already married," I

say. "We signed the papers three days ago." I swear all the oxygen gets sucked out of the room. A deadly silence is in the air, and both of my parents are staring at me in disbelief. They really didn't think that this was real.

"Are you serious?" my father asks.

"Yes." I let the information sink in.

"And her name is Monica Blast?" my mother asks. "Please don't tell me that it's the same Monica Blast that is the daughter of that monster." She looks at me with concern and pity, and I try not to be angry. I don't want pity.

She thinks that I'm doing this to satisfy some childhood dream. Maybe I was, but not anymore. "I know you thought you liked her when you were a kid, Daniel. But she was horrible to you. And you know what her family did to us. What would possibly possess you to do this?"

Because of the nature of what my family has gone through, we've always been able to be honest with each other. And so I decide to be honest with them. I tell them the truth: that I didn't expect to encounter Monica, and it started out as an endeavor for revenge. What quickly became apparent, is that neither Monica nor I were the same people that we thought the other one was. And that we were more well matched than we ever could have imagined.

So what started out as an endeavor of shame and humiliation, has turned into an endeavor of love. We haven't said it yet, but that's what I feel. I feel it in the silences in our conversations, and in the way we touch each other when we're not in the throes of passion. I feel it in the quiet moments when we don't have to talk to be comfortable. "I love her."

"No, you don't," my father says. "You can't possibly. There is nothing that woman could do to redeem herself for you.

Her family is responsible for nearly killing your mother. Is that not important to you?"

"Her father is responsible," I say. "Not her. She had nothing to do with it. For God's sake, she was a child, just like me. There's a lot about her life that you don't know, and it's not my place to tell you. But you of all people should know that money doesn't automatically make your life better."

My mother's face darkens with anger, and she stands, pacing the room. "I thought you were better than this, Daniel. I thought you were better than being sucked in by the Blast family once again. I thought that you, being the genius that you are, would see how poisonous they have always been. It doesn't matter if she's not directly responsible for what happened to us, she's still complicit. She bullied you for years. How can that not matter to you?"

"I never said that it didn't matter," I say. "I only said that I was able to move on. And if I, of all people, can move on and fall in love with her, surely you might be able to move on and see that she's not the horrifying monster that you think she is."

My father makes a face and a sound of protest. "I sincerely doubt that."

I'm not expecting the sudden anger, and I stand up, facing the two of them. "Honestly, I expected better from the both of you. If it was any other person—any other woman at all you didn't know—and I said that I had fallen in love and got married, you would have been happy for me. But instead, you're holding her accountable for crimes that she didn't commit. You've never even asked if she said she was sorry. Or wondered if she's a different person now. Do neither of you believe that people are capable of change?"

My father is the one that speaks first, though neither of

them speak immediately. "I remember watching your mother waste away with illness while we were sleeping in a car because condos and fancy restaurants were more important than the health of people living in that neighborhood. I remember seeing you come home ashamed, afraid, and downtrodden because she led a charge of bullying against you. I remember the terror and fear that it wasn't over, and that he would take more from us than he already had, simply because he could.

"And now I look at the news and I see him testifying, trying to get appeal and I know that he isn't sorry in the slightest. Why should I believe that his daughter is any different? Why should I think that she doesn't have some sort of personal stake in his release? How do you know you can trust her? How do you know she isn't just seducing you for your money, so that she can take it and run? Get back to the life that her family lost?"

"Your father makes an excellent point," my mother says. "I don't deny that people can change, Daniel. But we've lived longer than you have. And in my experience, they do not. Not when it comes to money. People are selfish, greedy, and they'll do whatever it takes to get ahead. No matter who they have to step on to do it. And the Blast family is the very worst example of that. So sure, people can definitely change. But in this case I highly doubt that it's true. You're being an absolute fool for trusting her, and I'm ashamed that you would do so."

It's then that I hear the smallest sound and turn to see Monica has stepped into the room. I don't know how long she's been standing there, but I know that I told her to come straight inside. For certain, she heard at least the last moments of my mother's diatribe against her. Probably more. The look on her face is stricken and broken, and all I can do is think: *dear God, what have I done?*

Everything freezes for just a second, and then I'm running, and so is she "Monica, wait!"

She's faster than I am, even in the heels that she's wearing. From what I can see, she looks beautiful, in a tasteful dark blue dress, dark hair curled.

I remember she was nervous to make a good impression, and I can't imagine how completely humiliated she must feel right now. I never meant for her to hear any of this. I never meant for them to even *say* any of it. In my wildest dreams I didn't expect this reaction from them.

I manage to make it to the front door, but by the time I'm there she's already outside. The car that dropped her off hasn't even left yet, and she's back inside before I can reach it. Running across my parents' front lawn, I'm desperate to get to the car door, but the car starts to move before I make it. I call after her, running after the car, but I know there's no point in that.

Pulling my cell phone from the pocket of my suit, I dial her number, but there's no response. After what she heard, I don't think that there would be. But this will not stand.

I stalk back into the house, filled with unholy rage. I don't remember ever being so furious at my parents before. My parents are good people. Solid people. I can't understate the amount of love that they've shown me in my life. I never want to make them feel like I don't appreciate them, and I understand more than most how deep this grudge can go. But to not even give somebody a second chance because of who their family is, it's utterly unacceptable to me.

I try to calm myself down as much as possible. I don't need to be driven by anger in this. I think anger will only make it worse. "I would like you both to explain yourselves," I say.

My mother looks a little stricken. And it is a moment before she speaks. "I'm sorry that she heard that, but it doesn't make what we said any less true."

"If you or Dad had committed a crime and gone to jail when I was in high school," I say, "would you want my life ruined, tainted by your own actions?"

I let those words sink in, so that they can see how ridiculous they're being. Monica was a teenager when most of these crimes occurred, despite the fact that they didn't come out until later. There is no excuse for blaming her for her parent's actions. "Because that's what you're doing. And frankly I don't care what you think. I love her, and I married her. If you can't accept that, I'm going to have to reevaluate *our* relationship. Believe me," I say, "I don't want to have to do that, but I will, for the sake of my marriage."

They look at me, and then they look at each other. I'm gratified to know that they look at least a little bit ashamed. But they say nothing.

"Will you at least meet her? Talk to her if she's even willing after what she just heard? Instead of condemning a woman that you barely know?"

They don't look happy about it, but both of them nod.

"Enjoy dinner," I say. "I need to go repair the damage that you've done."

My mother catches me before I reach the door, and pulls me into a hug. "I'm sorry," she whispers.

I can't say that I forgive her. Not yet. "If you really are sorry," I say, "prove it. Take a hard look at everything you said tonight. Let me know your decision." I do hug her back before I leave, because I love her. But right now, I need to find my wife. Because I need to tell her that I love her, and it can't wait another second.

## 14

# MONICA

I hold it together. I hold it together while I'm in the car, and I hold it together as I walk through the doors of the casino. Jack is the one who sees me, and sticks himself to my side as I enter. I hold it together as people take pictures, and I smile. But I don't go up to the suite. That's the first place that he's going to look, and I need some time. So instead, I go to the poker room. Jack doesn't even question when I go inside, standing outside the door and sealing me in.

It's then that I let myself go, and the tears come.

I got the text to come straight inside from Daniel. But I didn't know that when I walked inside, I would hear his parents giving voice to my worst fears. They think I'm a gold digger who's going to run away with his money. They think I'm a monster for what my parents did. They think that I'm seducing him for the sake of money and nothing else. And they are not wrong. I thought about giving into my father and sending him the money that he wanted.

But that would make me exactly who they think I am. I can't do it. I'll let myself be ruined, and I'll risk Daniel leaving me behind, but I won't do it. I love him. I can accept it now. I want to say it. I wish I had said it before I heard all of that. I know that he loves and respects his parents, and there's every chance that they'll get through to him. I don't want to think that it could be possible, but it is.

All that I want right now is to curl up into a bed and bury myself in blankets. But my situation hasn't changed, and I have nowhere to go. I suppose I could lock myself in the guest bedroom in the suite, but I don't want to do that. I'll just stay here for now.

The tears fall down my face, and I start to hiccup because I can't breathe. There's pain in my chest— an ache that I can't describe. I want to scratch it out and eliminate it. I want to tear it out of my chest and throw it far away. But I can't. It's the feeling of deep and utter betrayal. The knowledge that every horrible suspicion I had was true. The world sees me as evil, ruthless, a rotten apple by virtue of my terrible parents.

That makes the tears fall harder.

I sit down in the corner, pulling my knees up to my chest and taking off my shoes. It feels good to be small, and I press my head to my knees to make myself smaller. And I let myself cry. In a way, that feels good too, even though it hurts.

When the door opens, I know that it's him. I should have known that they wouldn't keep my location a secret for long. But they work for him, and not for me. I don't want to see him, and yet I want to see him so badly that it makes the tears flow fresh.

Daniel's footfalls are soft on the plush carpet, but I can still hear when he stops in front of me. "Princess?"

I squeeze myself further into a ball at the nickname. It feels childish, but I can't bear to look at him. I don't want to see his pity.

Hands brush my arms, move across my hair, stroking

down my sides. "Please, Monica," he whispers. "Please look at me."

I can't.

"I got there early to tell them about you and me," he says. "I never imagined that they would react that way. I thought that they would be happy for me. I never meant for that to happen, and I never meant for you to hear any of that. It's not true."

"Yes, it is," I say, finally looking up at him. My mascara is probably all over my face, and my eyes feel puffy enough that I have to squint. "It is true."

Daniel doesn't look betrayed, he looks exasperated. "What are you talking about?"

I duck my head down in between my knees again. "My dad called today. He wants your money. He promised me that he would ruin me if I didn't help him. He also promised that he would tell me where my mom is, if I just wired him a few hundred thousand dollars. And I thought about it. I actually thought about it. So, you see? They're right. Everything they said is true. You should hate me."

"I don't hate you," he said softly.

I push myself up to my feet and brush past him. "Don't you see, though? I almost robbed you. I don't deserve whatever love you ever had for me. I thought about helping a man who has already destroyed my life so thoroughly I didn't think it could recover. But I still thought I should help him. Because I didn't want to lose anything more. You won't be able to trust me again, and I understand. You'll never be able to know how bad I feel, but I understand whatever action you have to take."

Daniel stands slowly. "But you didn't do it."

"No," I say with a shuddering breath.

"So why wouldn't I be able to trust you? Why shouldn't I love you?"

I shake my head. "Because I thought about it. Because I'm my father's daughter, and his blood is in me. I have the same instincts. It's just a matter of time."

He takes a step forward, and I take one back. He takes another one, and I'm backed against the wall. This feels a little like déjà vu, because we were just here a few days ago in the same position. "You're not even hearing what you're saying, Princess," he says. "Your mind is twisted up because what my parents said is what you're afraid of. You didn't steal from me, and you didn't even want to. Your father black-mailed you. He used your mother against you, and your fear. Even if you had tried, it would have been his fault for making you feel like you couldn't. But you didn't. You told me." He leans close, not yet touching, but surrounding me. "And he won't touch you, I swear it. I can help you find your mother. I can make it so that his influence is nothing. You are mine, and I will protect you. That's the end of the story."

I shake my head. "You shouldn't trust me."

Daniel kisses me, and it undoes me. I'm crying again, but I so desperately want his kiss that I'm clinging to him too. "Who we were in the past doesn't matter anymore. That's what I'm trying to get through to my parents. That's what I've learned in these days with you. We are not the same people we were then, and our actions from that time do not have to define us. Our parents don't define us. We get to decide who we are now and what we want now. Right now, in this moment, I am a man who loves you. I am man who wants to be your husband, and give you everything. Who are you?"

Fresh tears fill my eyes, and I have to close them. "I am a

woman who loves you," I say, though my voice is shaking. "I want to be your wife."

Daniel's mouth crashes down on mine in a powerful kiss, taking me completely. There's no room for any other thought until he pulls away and leaves me gasping.

"Forget everything," he says. "Forget our history. Do you want me? Do you really want *me*?"

I look into his eyes, and at once, I know the truth. "Yes," I say. "But what about your parents? Do you really want to be with me if they hate me?"

"Yes." He presses his forehead to mine. "They're good people," he says. "But you know that forgiveness is complicated. They are going to come around. I'm absolutely sure that they'll love you the way I love you. And I love you so damn much, Princess. You are not to blame for the actions of your father. Eventually they'll understand that."

"Okay," I say.

"Do you believe me?"

I nodded. I do, but I can't help but worry. I don't want to be the thing that comes between him and his family. My own family has already done too much damage.

"Hmm," he makes a noise, pulling back to look at me. "I'm not sure that you do."

"I do, I swear."

His smile is gentle, but I see the gleam in his eyes. "I think I'm going to have to make sure that you understand how unequivocally I love you. And how much I want you." He leans close to my lips. "*I cannot get enough of you.*"

Daniel reaches down, and he grasps the hem of my dress, pulling it up, bunching it around my hips. He undoes his belt and pulls out his cock, already hard, and he lifts me off my feet like it's nothing. Like I'm a feather. And suddenly

I'm trapped between his body and the wall as he wraps my legs around his waist.

He slips into me like he's meant to be there, filling me up to the brim and taking my mouth again. He kisses me until I'm dizzy, and doesn't stop. I'm lightheaded when he releases my lips, chest heaving against his for air. "Do you believe that I want you?" he asks.

"Yes."

"I don't know," his voice is rough. "You don't sound convinced."

He thrusts upward into me, and I cry out. Fuck, yes. Arousal and pleasure and friction roll through me. I love this, and I love him. He fits with me the way no other person has. He sees all of me, even when I don't see myself. I don't think anyone else before him has ever seen me at all.

"Please," I tell him. "More."

"You don't have to fucking beg me," he breathes. "I want you to know that I want this. No strings attached. I want you forever, Monica."

I close my eyes and let the words sink in as he slows the rhythm down. Pumping into me smoothly and slowly.

He pushes me harder into the wall, so I'm absolutely pinned. Held in place by his hips and his cock. Impaled. He slides his hand up my neck and grips my hair. He loves grabbing my hair, and I've grown to crave the feeling of his fingers on my scalp. The guidance of his hands as he shows me where he wants me.

Right now, he tugs my head back, so I have no choice but to meet his eyes. I love his eyes, dark and filled with lust and more. Now I know that that unnamed emotion is love. I can see it there. He *loves* me.

That's what it takes for it to snap in. "Oh."

"There it is, Princess." He's smiling now as he kisses me.

He speeds up his rhythm again, slamming into me hard and fast. So deep and so fast that I can't breathe and I don't even care. My soul is settling, and my pleasure is rising. My husband loves me, and I love him. I *love* him. That's the end of it. Nothing else matters.

I'm going to come. I can feel it rising from deep within, vast and overwhelming. It rises so fast that I can't move or breathe, sudden pleasure overtaking my body and ripping through it. I scream into Daniel's mouth, releasing everything. Pain and grief and relief and pleasure. I gush over his cock, my orgasm soaking him.

He keeps fucking me, every bit of friction sending aftershocks through me and not letting me rest or breathe. It's like little bolts of lightning sparking all over me. The drop through the pleasure is sharp and sheer and I land on the other side with a moan. I've never had an orgasm like that, and I'm not sure I ever will again.

But that's not good enough for my husband. He pulls me away from the wall and suddenly, I'm back on my feet, Daniel bending me over the poker table. He strokes his hands down my ass, spreading me open before he plunges in again. I feel him against my back, leaning over me. He grabs my wrists and pins them to the table, and now we're lined up, body to body. His legs are against mine, arms on mine, back pinning me down, and cock, balls deep in my pussy.

"I love you, Monica," he says, thrusting deep. "I'm going to keep fucking you until you know."

"I know," I say, gasping. "I know. But please don't stop."

He chuckles, low and dark. "Never."

Daniel fucks me. And he doesn't hold back. Every ounce of strength and frustration and love and lust is powered into his movement. All I can do is take it. Another orgasm explodes through me, and I scream again. This one isn't muffled, and I don't give a shit. I'm seeing stars and rainbows and the whole damn universe behind my eyes as the pleasure burns me alive. And it doesn't stop.

Every thrust of his cock goes all the way to my core, and he grunts with every thrust. He's close, and I'm still there, coming over and over again until I think I'm drowning in it.

I feel it when he comes, burying himself to the hilt and pouring heat straight into me. I fall into one last orgasm, groaning as Daniel does too. We're falling together, and that's the point. We're together, and we always will be. I know it. I feel it.

We're both shaking and sweating now, and I'm not sure if my legs will support me. "Tell me you know," Daniel says, voice fierce in my ear. "Tell me you're sure."

He lets me up and pulls me with him, though he has to keep me upright. "I know," I say. "I believe you, and I love you too."

And an idea is brewing in my mind that I think he's going to love, and that might help smooth over things with his parents. "Good."

He tucks himself back into his pants, and helps me arrange my clothes. "Let's go."

"Where?"

He kisses me hard. "Upstairs. I don't plan on us sleeping for a long time, and we haven't eaten dinner. Maybe I'll eat it off you instead."

I laugh, because it feels so easy and so natural for Daniel to be tugging me toward the door and up to our suite. It feels perfect when he pins me against the elevator and continues to ruin my already ruined lipstick. And it feels like forever when we tumble into bed and get lost in each other again.

## 15

## DANIEL

"Yeah," I say. "That's perfect, thank you."

I hang up, and feel some measure of relief. That was the vineyard in Southern California where Monica and I have decided to host our wedding. Things were up in the air, but now it's finalized. Monica loves the venue, and I was willing to put a lot on the line to make it happen for her.

I'm sitting back at my desk, when I hear a knock at the door. I look over, and speak of the devil, it's my wife. I can't keep the smile off my face any more than I can keep myself in my chair. I spring up and I'm across the room before she can close the door behind her. I catch her in a kiss, and I love the way she melts into my arms. She kisses me back, and suddenly I wish that we weren't in my office.

It's only been a couple of days since the confrontation with my parents, and nothing has changed. I can't keep my hands off this woman, and I love her more than life itself. I reach down and hold her hands in mine, feeling for her wedding ring. "Hi, wife."

She's grinning when I pull away. "Hello husband."

"How are you?" I notice now that she has a package in

her hands. It's wrapped up like a gift, in bright blue paper. "What's that?"

"I'm good," she says. "I just saw the first sketches of the dress from Alex, and it's beautiful. And this," she says, holding out the present, "is for you."

"How's the dress?"

Monica rolls her eyes. "As if I'm going to tell you that. No bad luck."

I laugh. "I am hoping that you and I have had all the bad luck that we're going to have, Princess."

"Me too." She blushes. "Don't you want to open your gift?"

I pull Monica over to the couch in my office, and we sit together. "Why did you get me a gift?" I ask.

"I think that will be answered after you open it," she says.

And so I do. I tear off the paper and reveal a simple white box. Lifting the lid, absolutely everything goes still. It's like the world goes quiet for a second. Lying inside the box is a Game Boy.

But it's not just any Game Boy. It's the exact same kind. The same model I had that day when she tossed into the street.

The punch of emotion in my gut is not something I entirely expect. It brings up that memory, and the pain behind it. And though I've moved on, it's still a strong visual for me. "Why?" I ask.

"I can't turn back time. And you were right the other day when you said that our past actions don't define us. That they can't define us if we're ever going to move on. But it doesn't mean that I can't try to make things right. I know I hurt you that day. I know I hurt you a lot more than that day, and I'm sorry for that. I know it's not an excuse, but I was so far gone, so deep in that world that I didn't know just how awful I was being. I didn't know that until later.

"I got this for you as a reminder. Both for you and for me, that I can be better. Consider it my first step."

I haven't been able to look away from the toy, but her words drag my eyes to hers. "You've apologized more than enough, Monica. You know that, right?"

She nods, and I see the seriousness in her eyes. "I do know. But that doesn't alleviate all of my guilt. Neither does this. But I want to try."

I put the toy in the box on the table in front of me and pull her against me so that she's nearly in my lap. I kiss her, and I don't feel like I can stop. I kiss her until I feel like I'm going to pass out from lack of oxygen, and it's only then that I let go. "I love you, so much. And even though you don't need to apologize, and you don't need to feel guilty, I'm grateful for the gesture."

She blushes my favorite shade of pink, and looks away. I drag her gaze back to mine, and make her look at me. The fragile emotion I see there makes my heart skip a beat. I love to see that love in her eyes. I'm looking forward to seeing it on our wedding day. "How did you know? Which version to get? You actually remember that after all these years?"

Monica laughs, shaking her head. "Honestly, no. I didn't. So I went to the people that I knew would."

Shock strikes me. "You asked my parents?"

"I did."

I recognize the weight of the gesture now. It wasn't just about the Game Boy. It was about her reaching out to my parents regardless of their feelings about her. I haven't heard from them the last couple days, and I don't know their decision. In the end, it won't matter. I'm going to stay with Monica no matter what. But the fact that they spoke with her, and gave her the information that she needed, gives me hope. "That was brave of you," I say.

She smiles. "They were actually nice. When I explained what I needed and why I was doing it, they were more than happy to help. I think they may actually not hate me as much as they thought. We have a shot of getting them to come to the wedding."

I laugh, a laugh freer than I felt in a long time, because everything is absolutely perfect. I used to think my life was perfect, with my wealth and my job and having risen above my circumstances. But it wasn't. Now, with this gorgeous, brave woman in my life, it is.

I crush her to me, hugging her so hard that I feel her back crack and she makes a sound in protest. But then we're both laughing, and soon after that, we're kissing. I love Monica Blast, and I wouldn't have it any other way.

## One Month Later

I shouldn't be this nervous for my wedding to a man that I'm already married to, but I can't seem to escape the butterflies in my stomach. I've been ready for a while, but it's still a few minutes until the ceremony starts. I haven't seen Daniel since last night, and he's the only person I really want to see. So much has changed so quickly, but he's the only person who can ease this anxiety.

I want him to kiss me, and tell me he loves me like he does every morning now.

But anxiety aside, the wedding is going to be perfect. We are in a beautiful vineyard in Southern California. The weather is perfect, and I couldn't ask for a better setting for my wedding. Alex came through on the dress, and I've never felt as beautiful as I do now. It's gorgeous and flowing while at the same time comfortable and sleek and stylish.

There's a knock at the door, and I jump. "Come in."

The door opens, and Daniel's hand waves through. "I was told that I was not allowed to come in here without a blindfold," he says. "Alex threatened my manhood if I dared to look at the dress before the wedding, so I am here appropriately attired."

I laugh, and pull him into the room. True to his word, he's wearing a blindfold. "I swear, I won't tell if you don't," I say.

He grins. "Okay."

I pull his blindfold away, and he takes me in. His entire face goes slack, and his eyes are filled with awe. "You are absolutely stunning, Princess."

I love that that nickname started between us as his way of mocking me for being who I was. But over time it's come to mean more to us. I am his Princess, and he is my Prince. We are perfect for each other in every way.

"Thank you."

He leans forward and kisses me gently, and I know it's because he doesn't want to ruin my makeup. "I love you," he says.

I wrap my arms around him, and lean my head on his chest. It's hard to imagine myself any other place, since this has so quickly become my happy place. Just like I wished, I suddenly feel calm. "I missed you," I say. "I'm glad you risked Alex's wrath. But why did you?"

I can hear the smile in his voice even though I'm not looking at him. "Because I have a surprise for you. A wedding present of sorts."

"Before the wedding?" I look up at him and raise an eyebrow.

He nods. "I thought it would be better this way.

"All right."

Daniel kisses me again, soft and slow. "It'll be here in a

minute. I'll see you at the altar." He slips the blindfold back on again before he leaves the room, and I'm left wondering what the hell he's talking about. But true to his word, it's less than a minute later when a soft knock comes at the door.

I open the door, and I freeze.

Standing there, dressed for a wedding, is my mother.

After I confessed to Daniel that my father was black-mailing me, he hired the best private investigators in the country to find my mother, while making sure that she wouldn't be in danger. He also made sure that no further attempts at blackmail would be possible from my father. The story in the news now makes that clear. I don't think he ever thought that we would go public with his blackmail, but it killed any chance he had of an appeal, and the recording on the prison phone line is proof enough.

People still don't want to hire me because of my father, but it's not as bad as it used to be. I've made some connections, and hopefully after our long honeymoon, I'll be able to do some actual work.

My father was not invited to the wedding. In fact, he was banned from it in case he tried to leverage it for time free from prison.

But right now, I can't even think. Because my mother is here. "Mom?"

She smiles. "Hi, sweetie."

A thousand emotions go through me at once. Anger at her for abandoning me and being complicit to all those things my father did. Thankful that Daniel managed to find her, and fear of what will happen if my father finds out where she is. I don't know how much sway he still has over her. But also, I'm so fucking happy. I've missed her.

"What are you doing here?" I ask her.

She steps forward through the door and pulls me into a

hug. "Before I get to that," she says, "I need you to know that I'm divorcing your father. It took me a long time to figure out how to do it in a way that he would agree to. I didn't have any money of my own, and I know you didn't either. I never knew he did those things, I swear, Monica. If I had known, I would have left a long time ago and I would've taken you with me. I don't care what we would have done, as long as we wouldn't have had to be with him."

I hug her harder, because those are the exact words that I've been longing to hear.

"But to answer your question, I'm here because Daniel found me. He told me about the two of you, and I wouldn't have missed it for the world."

I hold onto her and I can't let her go. There's so much that I want to say, the words welling up in my chest until I can't say anything at all. I feel like I might cry, and my eyes well up, but she scolds me. "I'm not worth ruining your make-up over, dear. Your wedding is about to start. Don't worry about anything, we're going to have plenty of time to talk later. I just wanted you to know that I was here so that you didn't see me and get surprised during the ceremony. And I also want you to know I'm here when you say your vows."

"I love you, Mom." I know that I have things to work out with my mother. I know that we have things that we need to forgive each other for. But right now, those are the only words that matter.

"I love you too, Monica. Now go get married."

I smile at her, and it's genuine.

The wedding goes smoothly, and I cry like a baby during the ceremony. Thank God Alex made my make-up artist use waterproof mascara. The joy I feel absolutely takes me over the moon. Daniel is already mine, but now he's mine publicly. I can see it on his face, too. When he leans down to kiss me, I think I may explode with happiness.

The crowd cheers, and I know that I will remember this moment forever. In the moment after that, in the moment when we dance, and the moment when we cut the cake. The whole reception is a string of moments that are filled with perfect bliss. I chat with my mother. I dance with Alex. I kiss my husband, and lean against him when my feet get tired. I can't believe that this is my life, but I'm so happy that it is.

I never thought that I would be so happy about losing a hand of fucking poker.

It's already late in the night when Daniel and I decide to leave. We run to the car in a shower of sparklers, and kiss for the cameras while the guests cheer. I don't think I've ever been so exhausted and so happy at the same time. But I also know that our night is far from over. Because every time Daniel touched me today, I wanted him more.

In the month that we've been married, our craving for each other hasn't lessened in the slightest. Every night we fuck each other into exhaustion, and every morning one of us wakes the other up with pleasure. Except for last night and this morning, when we slept apart. And I can't wait to get back to our room so he can touch me.

Neither Daniel or I speak as we ride the elevator back up to our hotel room. We're staying in this resort for a couple of days before we leave on our honeymoon.

When we get to our bedroom, Daniel turns to me. "Have I mentioned today that I love you?"

I smile. "Several times, but I don't mind hearing it again."

"I love you." He pulls me against his body. "And I'm so happy that we had our wedding."

"Me too," I say, letting him kiss me. I kiss him back, our

tongues dancing, and letting that craving under my skin be unleashed. I fucking love it.

"I need to take advantage of this," Daniel says.

"Of what?"

That sharp, feral smile that I love so much comes out. "The opportunity to fuck my wife in her wedding dress."

I shiver at his words, and he sinks to his knees in front of me, lifting my skirt and disappearing beneath it. Daniel's hands run up my legs and pull them apart.

I'm wearing a white lace thong. Daniel's breath is hot on my pussy, and suddenly I'm clinging to the post on the bed to stay upright. There's a brush of his tongue on my clit, through the lace, and I moan. God, I'm soaking wet and he's barely touched me.

My husband has a talented tongue, and I love it when he uses it on me. His hands slide up to my hips and pull me closer, licking into me. He savors my clit through the lace, sucking deep. The rough texture of the fabric against my skin feels so good that I can't breathe.

But it's nothing compared to when he moves my panties aside and licks me again, his tongue sliding against my skin. Daniel sucks down to my entrance and back, and my knees are shaking. Sealing his mouth over me, he licks my clit, taking me higher and higher until I see white, almost ready to come. And then he's gone.

My orgasm fades, and I groan. "Why? Fuck."

Daniel lowers me down onto the bed, releasing his cock from his pants and hiking my skirt up so it's billowing fabric around the two of us. "Because I want you to come on my cock, Princess. I want to feel that pretty pussy squeeze me. Your first orgasm after your wedding is going to be me fucking you hard enough so you scream."

I try to focus on him, but my eyes won't focus as he slides

home, sending embers of pleasure spiraling along my limbs. "I always scream with you," I manage to say.

"And tonight will be no exception." His mouth crashes onto mine with beautiful, bruising force. His tongue plunges into my mouth, taking it with the same brutal momentum that he's fucking me with. He's not wrong. My lost orgasm is already back, bearing down on me with perfect certainty.

"Fuck," I say against his mouth, and Daniel goes faster, angling his hips in that perfect way that makes the stars flash behind my eyes, and my voice escapes me in a whine. I beg him. I gladly beg him to fuck me. I know that he loves to hear it, and I need it from him now. And so I beg.

The orgasm crashes down on me, crushing me with the pleasure of it. And I do scream. I scream his name. Yes. God. Yes. More. Fuck me, Daniel. And he does, yelling his own climax as he spills himself deep inside me.

His eyes devour me, watching me pant in my dress, still stuffed full of him. "We're not done, Princess," he says. "Once I get you out of that dress, we're going all night."

I grin at him. "And before you get me out of the dress?"

He stands, cock slipping out of me, slick from my pussy. "I think, Princess, that I'm going to need you to prove that you're an excellent wife."

Looking at his cock, my mouth starts to water. He's covered in our sex, and I want to taste it. I want to be on my knees for him in a way I've never wanted with any other man. I'll play this game. Because in the end, I love him and he loves me.

So I sink down onto my knees, my wedding dress puffing out around me, and I suck my husband's cock. I let him come down my throat while I'm staring up at him, and I let him peel me out of my wedding dress and fuck me again and again.

When we finally collapse together—sweaty and spent— even then we can't keep our hands off each other. Daniel pulls me to him and tucks me against his body. He kisses me softly, eyes closing. "I love you, Monica. Always."

I'm exhausted too, and I feel myself being pulled down into delicious, sated sleep. "I love you too," I say. I've never meant anything more.

www.ingramcontent.com/pod-product-compliance
Lightning Source LLC
Chambersburg PA
CBHW030311160726
47992CB00005B/1968